DISCARD

Acknowledgments

The end of a series means I have so many people to whom I owe my gratitude. I can't begin to remember them all. If you're holding this book, I hope you know you've touched my heart and changed my life. Thank you.

I would like to make special thanks to the people who helped edit and proofread: Rory Hume, Erin Conroy, Emily LaDouceur, Ashley Davis, and Melissa Miller, as well as Katja Rinne, who has been a helpful typo-pointer-outer and huge cheerleader.

And final, extra thanks to that husband guy for providing baby-wrangling services while I write/edit/everything else, as well as being delicious eye candy. I guess the part where you're an amazing partner and friend probably helps, too. But, you know, whatever.

DISCARD

Books by SM Reine

Everything is for Julian.
These books, my life,
and all my love.

Prelude

The Cage

A swollen moon crested over Gray Mountain. It was so huge and clear that Rylie thought she could reach out and brush its rocky face with her fingertips. Hazy silver halos radiated into the velvet sky. She stretched her hands toward it.

The moon called to her, telling her to change, and its song swelled in her heart. Her toes hung over the ledge. An inch forward, and she would fly away... or fall down the mountain.

"Rylie! Don't do it!" Seth scrambled over icy rocks, struggling to reach her at the peak.

A crack rang out as a rifle connected with the back of his skull. He collapsed at his mother's feet. Eleanor shouldered her gun again and aimed.

Dozens of gold eyes stared at them, reflecting the light of the full moon. Werewolves watched, waiting for Rylie to act, but a ring of hunters armed with silver bullets blocked them from reaching her. "Do it," Eleanor hissed. Sweat beaded her upper lip. "Call them!"

It was all too much: the rushing river, the wind through the trees, the howls of the wolves, and the call of the moon. Rylie had to act. Her time was up, and she needed to decide.

"Sorry, Seth," she whispered.

She stepped over the edge of the rocks.

One

The Gun

Sometimes, when Rylie was alone, she practiced shooting the gun. That was how she thought of it. Not "*a* gun," or "that pistol she stole from Abel," but *the* gun. Special emphasis on the first word.

It was a revolver. She knew this because the word was stamped on the side, along with the name of a manufacturer she didn't recognize. Rylie had never fired a gun before, but she had seen people get shot. After hours of turning it over in her hands, probing its parts with her fingertips, and pointing it at the wall, she thought she had it figured out.

She knew the business end and the trigger. Those were the important parts. Though not as important as the single bullet in the chamber.

Rylie sat on the edge of her mattress, popped the revolver open again, and tipped the bullet out onto her bedside table. It was the same lonely silver bullet she had been hiding in her room for weeks. It had been in the pistol when she stole it from Abel's duffel bag.

She warmed the metal of the gun in her hands, thinking about all the times she had seen Seth shoot empty cans and the way he stood to stabilize his arm. Rylie lifted the unloaded gun and aimed it at her wall. Pulled the trigger. Heard the *click*, watched the barrel rotate, imagined the resounding *bang*.

It wasn't cold in her room, but she shivered.

Her bedroom at the werewolf sanctuary was meant to be cozy. The walls were painted an inviting shade of blue, the bay window let her look down on the gardens, and her bed always had a fresh duvet filled with fluffy down feathers. But there was no hiding the fact that her window was barred from the inside, or that the paint was scored by claw marks. Her mattress had been replaced six times already, and she had only been there for four months.

Rylie aimed the gun at the claw marks on her wall. Those were from the last transformation, so Scott hadn't had time to repaint. He kept several buckets of that blue in the closet just for her.

Beyond the reinforced wall, Abel was waiting for the same thing that she was: a new moon. He changed later in the night than she did, so he might have been resting in anticipation. He would run with the other werewolves when the time came. They had acres of empty, fenced land to enjoy, where no human would be in danger.

Rylie wouldn't join them.

She pressed the barrel of the gun against her temple and closed her eyes.

Click.

Someone knocked on her door. Rylie shoved the gun under her pillow. "Come in," she said without raising her voice. Anyone visiting on the night of a new moon would have hearing as good as hers, and she could hear the mice playing in the field outside her window.

Abel entered. He was tall, dark-skinned, and broad-shouldered. He filled the room like shadows filled the night.

"What are you doing?" he asked. He wore nothing but loose linen pants, which were designed to fall apart when his body grew and changed. It bared the scars that ran from his temple to his hip.

"Same thing as you. I'm waiting."

His eyes narrowed. He sniffed. "What's that smell?"

The bullet was still on her table.

Rylie grabbed it when he peered out the window and tried not to wince at the way it burned in her hand. She sat on her fist. "I don't know. Did you bust into my bedroom to ask stupid questions, or is something going on?"

"Me and Bekah and Levi are leaving. We're taking the new kid out for her first run, so we thought you might want to come." He didn't manage to sound even slightly enthusiastic about the idea.

The "new kid" was Tyas, a thirteen year old who had fallen into their sanctuary after a family vacation to the Rockies ended in a werewolf attack. Her parents went home. She stayed. She had recently finished transitioning to a full werewolf, spoke very little English, and cried all the time. Rylie had been avoiding her. Actually, she had been avoiding everyone, but Tyas more than the others.

"No thanks," she said.

Abel glared. "You're changing in here again?"

"So what if I am?"

"We've got two hundred acres out there, and you haven't seen more than the front yard. I know you're still being all whiny about that thing that happened at Christmas—"

"Whiny?" Rylie's voice went up an octave. She couldn't hold it back. "You think being upset about killing eight people is *whiny*?"

He shrugged. "I've killed more than that."

"You've killed werewolves. Not farmers. Not fathers. Not—"

"Whatever. Look, you can stay in here if you want. I don't care if you want to mope in your gloomy pit of a room. But Bekah's getting worried that you won't leave, and that means

Scott's getting worried, too. You're going to have a whole coven of witches on you if you don't act like you're getting better."

She bit her bottom lip. "But I'm not getting better."

"Like I said. Whatever." Abel paused halfway out her door, and something flitted across his face that might have been sympathy. "You and me could go on our own. You know, let Bekah and Levi babysit Tyas. There's plenty of space."

"No," Rylie said forcefully.

Any hint of kindness vanished from his expression. Abel's mouth opened like he was going to say something else, then clapped shut again. He slammed the door behind him. It was reinforced with silver and steel, so it clanged in the frame.

Rylie peeled her fingers open. The bullet had burned a red divot into her palm. She grimaced as she slid it into the chamber of the revolver, then blew on the injury and shook out her hand.

She wasn't whining or moping, no matter what Abel said. She was more dangerous than the other werewolves at the sanctuary. It was better to hide.

Rylie tucked the gun into a drawer on her bedside table. Her blood grew cold as she closed it, and her gaze was drawn to the window. The new moon was invisible in the black sky, but she knew it was peeking over the hill. She could always feel the moon.

The change tugged at her, like the moon was connected to her breastbone by a silver thread. Rylie stood and grabbed the bars as she gazed out at the clear night sky. Her heart worked twice as hard to beat. Her blood grew thick and sluggish.

Almost time.

She fastened the bar on her door—not that werewolves were any good at operating doorknobs—and undressed. She folded her clothes and stuck them in the drawer with the revolver. Her hands shook as she pushed her furniture against the walls.

"Maybe it won't hurt this time," she whispered.

The stars blurred as the moon rose. Her eyes burned with tears. Her skin itched with fever.

Figures darted past the window. Four other werewolves, still in human form, fled for the trees. The wolf inside of Rylie longed to join them. She wanted to run, to feel the dirt between her toes, to be enveloped in the chilly spring breeze.

Someone gave a sad cry that sounded like a howl. They wanted her to come, too.

No. I can't.

The last time she ran loose, she'd almost killed her aunt.

Painful memories were enough to kick the change into high gear. The power of the moon buckled her knees. Rylie sank to the floor and her forehead bumped against the carpet.

Her jaw and cheekbones popped. Her skull cracked like ocean ice as her muzzle grew, and the skin stretched to the point of tearing. Rylie's nose extended in front of her eyes as teeth erupted in her gums with flares of pain. Blond hair pooled around her hands.

It shouldn't have hurt. After so many months of shifting shapes, she should have been used to it. But it was like taking a sledgehammer to the face every time.

She cried out as her lower back snapped, flinging her onto her side. Her kneecaps dislodged. Her anklebones strained as her feet rearranged.

The room blurred. She couldn't focus on anything but the carpet two inches from her face. Where was the wolf? She prayed for it to sweep her human mind away and release her from the pain.

Let me go... let me forget...

The tail ripped free of her back. New muscles knit together as fire swept down her spine.

The mind of the wolf pressed into her, and Rylie surrendered. The pain became distant. It kept her from having to think about murders, revolvers, or monsters. And she definitely didn't have to think about everything she had left behind when the werewolf destroyed her life.

All she knew was the cold peace of a predator's mind. It was better that way.

Two

Peaks and Valleys

At some point, Rylie fell asleep. And she had that dream again.

She stood on the shore of a wide, glistening lake. The sun was gold with the haze of summer, mosquitoes clouded the glistening water, and something moved on the opposite shore. If Rylie turned, there would be cabins behind her, and giggling girls running to the next activity. It would be archery again. It was always archery on Wednesday afternoons.

But she couldn't turn from the mountain. She squinted at the peak, trying to see it through the ring of clouds and sunshine. There was something moving through the rocks up there. It was waiting for her.

A cold wind almost knocked her into the water. Rylie staggered. Her foot connected with something soft and wet.

There was a body face down in the sand. She didn't have to roll it over to recognize those long silver braids and frail shoulders.

No. It can't be.

The gale pushed again. She raised a hand to shield her face from the showering pine needles as her hair was blasted back from her face.

There weren't any cabins or laughing girls behind her. Instead, there was a line of trees that had grown so close together that the sun couldn't pierce the canopy of branches. It was always night in the forest, even on the warmest and sunniest of days.

Wolves howled. They were deeper in the woods, and they wanted her to join them.

Water lapped at her ankles. The tree branches bent toward her. She spun in a circle, searching for an escape, but the mountain was everywhere. It was everything.

And it wanted her.

Shock jolted Rylie awake. Her eyes flew open, and her heart pounded in her chest. Her body was drenched in sweat.

She was also on the floor.

The carpet was spotted with drying blood. Fistfuls of white-gold hair were clumped by the wall. Nobody had come in to clean yet.

Rylie grimaced at the window. The sun was high in the sky, and Abel leaned against the bars. That could only mean one thing: it was the morning after the new moon. He always visited her when she woke up.

"Took you long enough," he said.

Squinting through the sunlight, she could see that Abel looked way too awake and refreshed for the morning after a moon. He smelled like shampoo. Even though his eyes were rimmed with circles, he was actually standing up and fully clothed, which was more than Rylie could say. His beard was even trimmed.

He was also chewing a huge, barely-cooked steak. Her empty stomach gnawed beneath her ribs. "Ugh," she groaned.

"Yeah. Good morning to you, too. I brought a present." He pointed to the floor, and she noticed a second plate next to the shredded remains of her bed. She was going to need a new mattress again.

She fell on her breakfast, ripping into it with dull human teeth. "How long have you been up?" she asked around a juicy bite of meat.

"Since dawn. It's almost three now." Abel swallowed the last of his steak and sucked the juice off of his fingers. Rylie was afraid to ask how much of that time she had spent furry. It was normal for werewolves to change back at sunrise, but she hadn't been normal for months. "You turned back at noon. I know you're wondering."

No wonder she was so tired. Judging by her furniture, the wolf must have been trying to escape all day.

"Thanks," she said.

"Uh huh. Food's not the only thing I have for you. I'll be back in a minute."

Abel left, and Rylie took the chance to hurriedly dress in shorts and a t-shirt before finishing breakfast. Even though he had given her a hunk of cow that weighed at least two pounds, she was still starving when the bone was bare.

She contemplated her dream as she sucked on the remaining rib. It wasn't the first time she had dreamed about Gray Mountain. That was where she had been bitten almost a year earlier, so it was serious nightmare fuel. But Rylie had stopped dreaming completely since she got silver poisoning. The wolf occupied her sleeping mind.

Did that mean that the beast was the one having nightmares?

Voices crossed outside her window. She dropped the bone on her plate and peeked through the bars.

Levi and Scott were conversing down the hill. She could have made out their words if she focused, but considering how upset they looked, Levi was probably complaining about Rylie's behavior again. She didn't want to hear about how much she needed drastic intervention for the twelfth or thirteenth time. It was like a popular song on the radio: kind of entertaining at first, but it got on her nerves after a few weeks.

Her stomach grumbled. She checked the time. Three o'clock, like Abel said. There was always a witch in the building to keep an eye on the kids—usually Scott, when he wasn't pulling the traveling psychiatrist routine—and they prepared food at the same time every day. Three o'clock was between meals. She could steal another steak from the kitchen without seeing anyone.

Abel met her outside the door to his room. "Going somewhere?"

"Food."

"Sounds good. I'll come."

He matched her pace, and Rylie noticed he had something in one of his hands. Her heart sped. "Is that...?"

He held up an envelope. The sharp handwriting spelled out her name. "What, this little letter? You're not excited about it, are you?"

"Give me that," she said, holding out a hand.

"Hmm." He tapped the corner against his chin. "I don't know..."

Rylie shoved him against the wall and snatched it from his hand. Being the older werewolf gave her the advantage in strength, even though she was a foot shorter. He didn't try to fight back.

She hugged the letter to her chest. It smelled faintly of gunpowder and leather.

Abel gave an exaggerated eye roll. "You two make me sick. Are you ever going to write back to him?"

Rylie bit her bottom lip. Her boyfriend, Seth, had sent a letter every week since she moved into the sanctuary. Sometimes two a week. It wasn't always a long note, since his life had become boring after all the werewolves left, so sometimes he included drawings or pressed leaves from the orchard instead.

It made her heartsick to think of him. She only read the letters in her bedroom, just in case the emotions were too strong to control and she transformed. It had happened twice already.

She couldn't imagine writing back. She hadn't even said goodbye.

Cheeks burning and lips sealed, Rylie focused her eyes on her feet and didn't reply. Abel ghosted behind her through the halls without trying to provoke her again. It was rare for him. He loved to annoy her. But he could also be very quiet, for such a big guy.

Probably from all those years he spent hunting werewolves.

The house was empty after the moon. Their footsteps echoed off the stairs as they headed through the archway into the kitchen. Everything was red tile and glossy marble countertops. The witches had hung a big pentacle on one wall and put fresh herbs in the window to dry. Passing the icon made her skin crawl. Scott had told her a dozen times that it had nothing to do with Satanism, but she still didn't like it.

Abel was eyeballing the pentacle, too. "Want to take that thing out back and set it on fire?"

"Sure, if you want to be the one who touches it. Who knows what kind of curses it has?"

He grimaced. "Point taken."

They raided the fridge together, which was mercifully occult-free aside from a group photo of the coven with a big "Blessed Be!" stamped across the bottom. Scott was on the right side with his arm looped around his daughter, who was a taller, strawberry-blond, and somewhat less Sean Connery-looking version of her dad. The other witches were middle-aged women called stupid things like Broomstick and Thistle.

The refrigerator was full of thawing steaks and chicken limbs. There was always some combination of raw meat available. Feeding five teenage werewolves was no small feat, and they were careful to make sure that the kids never went hungry.

"Maybe if I used thick gloves," Abel mused while they waited for the oven to heat their food to body temperature. He was still glaring at the giant pentacle.

Once everything was cooked, Rylie and Abel sat at the dining room table to eat. It looked out on a patio where Scott had placed chairs and a ping-pong table so the kids could have fun on their human nights, but Rylie never used it.

"How was the new moon run?" she asked between mouthfuls of steak.

He shrugged. "Boring. The way they like it."

"So Tyas is adjusting?"

"You could call it that," he said with a snort. "She ate a deer. I grabbed a few bites myself. It wasn't bad, you know. Fresh venison."

She winced. "Don't tell me about it. Please." Rylie had once been an avid vegetarian. Once she'd seen how livestock was slaughtered, she had lost her stomach for dead animal flesh. But a werewolf's need for meat was more than preference. She would go wild if she tried to starve herself.

Abel grinned. "Bet you don't want to hear about the part where I woke up with deer fur stuck in my teeth."

"Seriously, shut up."

"I can't believe you still have a weak stomach for deer."

Her cheeks flamed again, and she stared hard at the pattern left by the grease on her plate. "Yeah, well, I can't believe I put up with you."

"Nobody else can bring you Seth's letters." He shrugged at her nasty glare. "Just saying."

"Jerk," she muttered under her breath.

"Emo kid."

She threw her plate in the sink and very deliberately did not touch the sprayer. There was a sign on the wall written in Bekah's tidy cursive that said "Rinsing your dishes makes the dishwasher happy!" surrounded by lots of hearts.

"Hey!"

Levi slid through the doorway on socked feet, catching himself on the counter.

She rolled her eyes. "Are you the dishes police now, too? Are you going to yell at me for leaving dirty plates in the sink?"

"What? No." He had to stop between words to take a breath. His honey-brown hair, darker than his sister's but no less curly, was frazzled and sticking up in every direction. He looked like he had been running for miles. It wasn't easy to exhaust a werewolf.

"What's going on?" Abel asked, entering the kitchen.

There was no color in Levi's face. "Bekah is gone."

•○•

Levi searched as a wolf with Abel close behind, but Rylie kept her investigation closer to home.

She searched in Bekah's favorite hiding spots first. Bekah wasn't in her bedroom. She wasn't tending to the tomato sprouts that were getting hardened off in the shed. She also hadn't curled up with a book in the so-called "study," which had three bookshelves behind two televisions and four different video game consoles.

The other girl hadn't been in the sanctuary for hours, as far as Rylie could tell. All her smells were old.

Scott fretted while everyone else searched. When Rylie finished looking around, she found him trying to call Bekah's cell phone for what had to be the millionth time. It had been a whole hour since Rylie had eaten, so she snagged some beef jerky out of the pantry while she watched him pace.

Watching him hang up and dial again and again got painful after a few minutes. Rylie interrupted him. "I don't think she's here."

"Hope springs eternal," he said. "You kids are never far from your cell phones."

"Yeah, but wolves don't have thumbs."

His brow was pinched. "Why would she still be a wolf?"

Rylie shrugged. If Bekah was distant enough to elude her sense of smell, then she was probably traveling on all fours. But

Scott didn't seem to accept that she might be gone. Really gone.

"I'll check her room for a note," Rylie said. They had already looked for her in there three or four times, but the suggestion took the edge of fear off of Scott's smell, so it seemed as helpful as anything else they could do.

He kept trying to call Bekah as they went to her room. When they got to the hall outside her door, Rylie's ears picked up a buzzing sound.

She went inside. Where Rylie's bedroom was like an especially nice prison cell, Levi and Bekah's rooms were normal bedrooms. They weren't at risk of transforming between moons, so the window wasn't barred. Bekah had a shaggy rug in the shape of a flower. Her easel had a blank slate of paper. Her bed had a cute comforter patterned with ivy and roses. They had tried to give Rylie a similar comforter, but she had eaten it.

"Call Bekah again," she said, and he obeyed.

The glow of a cell phone vibrating under Bekah's dresser caught her eye. She picked it up. Thirty-four missed calls weren't exactly a million, but it was pretty close.

Scott swore under his breath.

But the cell phone wasn't the only thing under the dresser. Rylie pulled out a piece of paper, and then another, and another. Bekah had hidden stacks of paintings behind the furniture where nobody would have thought to look.

"What is that?" he asked.

She sat back, spreading the pages around her on the carpet. Watercolors warped the papers, giving texture to every peak and valley Bekah had painted. Each image was nearly identical. Yellow lights were picked out at the base of a tall mountain, like a distant town—or a forest full of cabins.

"Camp Silver Brook," Rylie whispered.

There was no way Bekah had ever been to Gray Mountain. None of the other werewolves had. They were on the opposite side of the country, and both youth camps had been closed since a werewolf attack killed several people. Only Rylie had survived being bitten.

Rylie smelled Levi and Abel approach before they showed up in the doorway.

"She's not on the grounds," Levi said, putting on a shirt. The laces on his linen pants were still loose. "I found her smell on the road out of here, but it disappears in the forest."

"Look at this," Scott said, lifting one of the paintings. It was the same peak from another angle. "Do you recognize the subject?"

"That's it," Levi said. "That's the mountain I told you about."

"What mountain?" Rylie asked.

Scott frowned at a third painting. "Levi has been having strange visions."

"Dreams," he interjected.

"Visions. Dreams. Call them what you will. He's been seeing the same mountain repeatedly, and so has Tyas. She began having these dreams after her last moon, when she assumed the true wolf form, and we realized they were 'dreaming' about the same place when they both said the visions had cabins." Scott swallowed hard. "But Bekah never mentioned..." He set the pictures down and took a deep breath to steady himself.

Abel's voice broke through the stunned reverie. "Look at this."

He fished a diary out of the space behind Bekah's dresser and handed it to Rylie. The first pages were covered in her normally tidy handwriting, but halfway through, it turned virtually unrecognizable. "I have to get there," she read out loud. "Have to get there, have to get there... That covers, like, three whole pages. And then 'they need me' covers another three pages."

"She went crazy," Abel said.

Levi jerked the diary out of her hands. "Bekah's not crazy!"

"Well, the answer is obvious," Scott said with a distant, pensive stare. "We don't know why, but we know where she's gone. That gives us a place to begin searching."

Rylie felt like the ground was breaking up beneath her feet.

Gray Mountain.

The despair and fear that swelled within her was too much. The wolf didn't care about searching for Bekah, but it cared about the place it had been born. And worse, Rylie cared about it, too. She felt the massive, furred body of the wolf surge inside her. It rubbed against the inside of her throat.

She shoved past Abel and ran to her room, slamming the door shut behind her.

Three

Open House

A warm wind rippled through the long grass outside of the Gresham ranch. It tasted like oncoming summer—the first breeze without the bite of winter's cold in months. A lone white cloud drifted over a hill dotted with violet blossoms.

Dust kicked up behind a steel blue Chevy Chevelle as it turned off the highway and bumped up the road to the ranch house. It slowed by the mailbox. The window rolled down.

Seth reached out an arm to remove a handful of envelopes. The engine idled as he sat back to flip through them.

He had brown skin, brown eyes, and brown hair, which he had been growing out and had straightened so that it reached his jaw. His skin had gotten even darker since he quit the football team and dedicated his time to working on the ranch instead. It seemed like the least he could do, since Gwyn was letting him stay with her until he graduated high school in three weeks.

"We're reaching record highs this spring!" the radio announced. "It got up to eighty-eight degrees yesterday, which is the warmest first week of May we've seen since the year 1865. That is crazy. Don't you think that's crazy, Bill?"

"Crazy good!" Bill drawled. "And the horses are *loving* it. I got to take Old Blue out for her first good run this season…"

Seth turned the radio down and the car's fan up.

He glanced through the stack of envelopes. Hospital bills. Advertisements from the Realtor's office. The weekly specials from the grocery store. And another hospital bill. There were no letters from Rylie, and nothing from any of the universities he had applied to. Twice the disappointment, but nothing new.

He tossed the mail onto the passenger's seat and drove the rest of the way to the ranch house.

There were three cars waiting by the door into the kitchen, which was how everybody got into Gwyneth Gresham's house. He couldn't remember the last time someone had opened the front door. One of the trucks belonged to the gardener they hired to beat the orchard into shape, one was the Realtor's, and the third was a black SUV that Seth didn't recognize. It must have belonged to one of the prospective buyers for the ranch.

He could make out figures moving through the freshly washed windows of the barn. The Realtor was working her magic.

Seth kicked the mud off his boots before entering the kitchen.

Aunt Gwyn sat on a stool by the counter as she arranged tulips in a ceramic vase. Even though it was over eighty degrees again, she was wearing a long-sleeved shirt and hat inside. She was self-conscious about all of her bruises. "Hey, son," she greeted Seth as he handed her the mail. "How was school?"

"It was all right."

"All right?" She narrowed her eyes. He could feel the weight of her gaze on the back of his neck as he filled a glass with filtered water. "Sounds mighty ominous."

Seth forced his features into a solemn mask and took a long drink before responding. "Yeah. I got to see my grades."

Gwyn set the scissors down and folded her hands. Her thick gray braids were undone, leaving her hair in looping curls over her shoulders. Combined with her heavily lined face, she looked like a very stern old wise woman. "Tell me you at least got an A on your term paper."

"I did," he said as seriously as possible. Then he couldn't hold it back anymore. His mouth split in a huge grin. "And I've got A's on everything else, too!"

She gave him a dirty look that didn't hide the warmth radiating from her eyes. Her cheeks dimpled. "You had me going there for a minute."

"It gets better. The school counselor said I've done so much extra credit that I'll pass all my classes with A's, even if I flunk finals!"

Gwyn flung her hands in the air and gave a whoop. "Damn, boy, you don't do things halfway! Come here, come here."

Seth bent down and let her give him a hug. Her body was frail, but she wasn't quite as gaunt as she had been around the New Year. Her embrace warmed him in a way that had nothing to do with record highs. He had never been congratulated for good grades before moving in with Gwyn. She made him feel like a superhero.

"Thank you," he said, planting a kiss on her temple.

"Ah, shut up. You're making me all mushy." She swatted him on the shoulder. "Get out of here and find something useful to do, Einstein."

"You kidding me? I'm not doing anything useful for the next month." He flopped onto the stool next to her.

"You've still got to finish the year out."

"I know, I know." His smile faded. "Have we gotten any calls today?"

Gwyn cleared her throat and went back to trimming stems. "Only from folks wanting to see the ranch."

It was hard to feel too happy when they hadn't spoken directly to Rylie in months. She had only called once, all the way back in February, and it was to ask her aunt about how treatments were progressing. She refused to speak to Seth. He did hear from Abel every Monday and Thursday, and he got secondhand updates about Rylie that way, but it wasn't the same.

"I still haven't heard back from any of the universities," Seth said, which was only fractionally less depressing than his girlfriend's refusal to speak with him.

"Bet things are just going slow."

Seth bent a flower's stem in his fingers. "Maybe I'm that terrible. Maybe nobody wants to touch me."

Gwyn snorted. "Sure, wonder boy. You and all your perfect grades are so damn offensive that nobody will dare respond to your applications. I'm convinced. Tell you what: I'll make some calls tomorrow and see what's going on. All right? But you can't sit around. I told you to find something useful to do, and I meant it."

Seth gave an exaggerated groan. "Fine. How's the orchard going?"

"Dunno. You can check on the gardener when the Realtor's done showing the newest lady around."

"Is this one actually going to make an offer?"

Gwyn shrugged. "Heck if I know. I've got plenty else to concern myself with." She plumped the flowers up and tilted the vase to examine it from another angle. "What do you think? Pretty nice, huh?"

"It's... flowery."

"Yeah, yeah. Get outside."

Seth drained his glass of water, put it in the sink, and headed outside. He grabbed one of Gwyn's spare hats on the way out and checked the weeds sprouting next to the steps. He had sprayed weed killer on them twice, but they kept coming back. Pulling them would be productive, but it was too hot.

Plopping the straw fedora on his head, he stretched out on the hood of the Chevelle. The glass was warm beneath his back as he reclined on the windshield.

It would be a great time for a nap, ut he didn't close his eyes. He tipped his hat down to shade his face and leaned around to grab his binder from the passenger's seat. Seth flipped it open to blank piece of paper and chewed on his pen for a minute before writing.

Rylie,

Spring's here. You'd like it. There's flowers blooming, and Gwyn's on a cleaning frenzy. Getting stuff done makes her so happy.

And you know, graduation is coming up. I've got such good grades that I'm definitely walking even if I blow my finals. It's hard to believe I made it. I didn't think I ever would. But even though I'm getting ready to graduate, it's not as good as I expected.

Not without you…

Feet crunched on the dirt. Seth pushed the brim of his hat back to watch the Realtor return to her car. The prospective buyer was hidden behind her.

He folded the letter and tucked it in his back pocket, pretending not to listen to their conversation. "You should really see it at night," the Realtor said with all the enthusiasm of an artist sharing her masterpiece. "You can come back this evening if you want to see more. The fireflies…"

"I've seen enough."

Every muscle in Seth's body turned to stone.

He didn't want to turn around. As long as he didn't see her, he wouldn't have to admit to himself that he knew that voice. There was no way she had the nerve to come back. Not after what she did to Rylie.

The Realtor said her goodbyes and drove away, leaving him alone with the buyer.

He slid to the ground and faced her.

If vipers could grow two legs and walk among humans, Eleanor would have been their queen. She was tall, muscular, and mercilessly beautiful. Her hair was slicked back. Her shoulders were straight. She wore her usual uniform of a black tank top and cargo pants, although she had thrown a shirt over it to make her look fractionally less military.

Eleanor didn't smile for Seth.

"Hello," she said.

He removed the fedora and held it to his chest. "Mom. What are you doing here? You can't tell me you want to buy the ranch. You couldn't even afford it."

"You don't know anything about me, boy," Eleanor said with venom in her voice.

Seth thought about the guns in the house. He had only kept one—his favorite rifle—and it was locked in a living room cabinet, since Gwyn didn't want weapons in his bedroom. It was too far away. Knowing his mom, she had at least two knives and a handgun somewhere on her body.

He inched toward the kitchen door. Annoyance flitted through Eleanor's eyes. "I didn't come back to buy the ranch, and I didn't come back to fight you. Stop thinking about running."

"I've stopped running. You're the one who left."

Eleanor folded her arms. "And it looks like I'm not the only one who did. Where's that blond tramp? What happened to your happily ever after?"

"Not to disrespect, *Mom*, but that's none of your business."

"It's fine. You don't have to tell me. I know where she is."

Sudden fear for Rylie made him raise his fists, but a single look from Eleanor made him freeze in his tracks. Nobody did icy stares like his mom. "Leave her alone," he growled.

She glanced at her watch, unimpressed by his threat. "I'm almost out of time. Listen to me, boy: I've got a new family now. A better family. And I've come to bring you into the fold." She swept a hand to the black SUV. "See what I've got? That's just the beginning. They've given me money, a home, a purpose. They're called the Union. It's a whole army of men like you and your daddy."

Seth's father had been what was called a kopis—the latest in a long line of people who hunted supernatural creatures. His dad, and their entire family, specialized in taking down werewolves. Being a little stronger and faster than most humans gave them the edge. An army of them could be bad. Really bad.

"What purpose did they give you?" he asked.

"Werewolves are on the move all around the world. They're converging." She said the last word carefully, like it was a vocabulary term she had recently learned.

"Why?"

"The *why* doesn't matter. This is our chance." Eleanor shook her fists with barely restrained anger. "The werewolves took everything from us. They took your daddy's life and ate his spleen, they mauled your brother, and they took you from me, too. Now they're going to all be in the same place, and me and the Union team are going to kill them. All of 'em."

"Are you kidding? There's got to be thousands of them."

She smiled a nasty smile. "Barely a hundred. This is the end, and we've almost won. All we've got to do is one final hunt."

"Where's the convergence?"

Eleanor seemed to take his question to mean that he wanted to go. Her smile turned triumphant. "Gray Mountain."

It made sense in a sick way. That was where it had all begun. The legends said that the animal gods had descended on the mountain to give humans the ability to shapeshift. That was where Jericho had tried to start his pack, and that was where Rylie's life as she knew it had ended.

"We've already got a team waiting there, but I came back for you." Eleanor spread her arms wide, like she was offering a hug to him. He couldn't remember ever having hugged his mom before. Not even in his earliest memories. "Let's be a family again."

"It takes more than blood to be family," Seth said.

Anger clouded her expression. "You ungrateful little punk."

Gwyneth emerged from the house. Her hat hung over her back, and she cradled a shotgun in the crook of her arm like a baby. In the sunlight, her skin looked a fraction too pale, and her hair was more frazzled than usual. But her confident stride didn't betray her weakness. She braced her feet a short distance up the hill. "I'm pretty sure the boy wants you to leave him alone."

She didn't aim the gun, and she didn't have to. Eleanor took a big step back, keeping both Seth and Gwyn in her sights. Her hands hovered at her hips like an Old West gunslinger.

"Stay out of what's none of your business, Gresham," Eleanor growled.

"You okay, Seth?" Gwyn called. He nodded. "You want this woman gone?"

He hesitated. His mother glared at him, making it clear that he had better give the right answer if he didn't want to deal with it later. "Yeah," he said. Eleanor looked like she had been slapped.

"You're making a mistake," she said.

Gwyn pumped the shotgun. "You heard him."

Eleanor glared with black hatred, but she didn't argue. She paused before getting in the SUV. "I'll be at the motel another night if you change your mind."

He shielded his eyes from the sun and watched her drive down the hill to the highway. Gwyn unloaded the shotgun behind him. "What was that about?" she asked, pocketing the shells.

"She said all the werewolves in the world are converging in one place. She's going to try to kill them."

"Would 'all the werewolves' include Rylie and Abel?"

"Yeah. It would."

"Then we better go save them," she said, and she went inside to prepare.

Four

The Plan

Once Rylie had control of her wolf again, she opened the door to her bedroom. Abel was seated on the floor outside as he oiled a handgun. "Having fun?" she asked, slipping out and shutting the door so he wouldn't see how much damage she had inflicted on her bed.

"Oh, yeah. This whole Bekah thing is great. You know how I love hunting wolves." He dropped his rag and got up. "So what were you doing in there? Did you change?"

Rylie glanced at the blood caked around her nails. "Nope. Just took a quick nap."

"Uh huh. Come on. The coven's gathered while you were 'sleeping.'"

"What for?"

Abel rolled his eyes. "Planning."

Usually, the coven liked to meet in the back of the fields. Rylie asked why they would do that when the house had a lot of big, empty rooms, and Scott gave her a dumb answer about connecting with the mother goddess through the Earth and trees and hearing her wisdom on the breeze. But they didn't seem to need her windy wisdom that day, because they met in the sheltered patio area instead.

Only Thistle, Blackbird, and Scott's daughter Stephanie were able to attend. Everyone was gathered around the table except Tyas, who was hunched on the back step crying again. Rylie could count the number of times she had seen the younger girl smile on one hand.

Rylie dragged a chair to the corner of the patio, where she hoped she wouldn't have to be involved with the meeting. Abel stood at her side. He was almost as bad at being a team player as she was.

"Looks like we're all present," Scott said. "We can get started."

"What about Bekah?" Stephanie asked. Scott's daughter was a prim, rigid woman wearing a white lab coat and drumming her fingernails on the arm of her chair. She had never taken a shift at the sanctuary. She didn't seem to know how to be friendly, much less take care of a house full of teen wolves.

"Bekah is gone. She disappeared last night."

The witches gasped. Thistle got pale and had to grab the table to keep from falling over. She was a plump woman with graying hair who spent her shifts at the sanctuary baking cookies, weaving dream catchers, and ranting about spirit journeys.

"Is she okay?" asked Blackbird.

Scott rubbed a hand down his face. "I hope so. We only have theories about where she's gone."

"Gray Mountain," Levi said, pointing at a giant map of the United States he had put on the table. He had marked possible routes from the sanctuary to the mountains in permanent marker. "Twenty-five hundred miles away. If you drive without stopping, it's a three-day drive. But none of the cars are missing, so Bekah's not driving."

Thistle managed to gather her composure. "Isn't Gray Mountain the place the kids have been seeing in their visions?"

"Dreams," Levi corrected.

Scott nodded. "It's an important location in the mythology surrounding werewolves. They say it's where it all began. I don't know why they would have visions about it—sorry, Levi—but it must mean something."

She focused on her hands in her lap. Just hearing the name of the mountain was enough to get the wolf stirring again.

Don't feel anything. Don't think. Don't lose control.

"We don't have any time to lose. If Bekah is traveling as a wolf, she could already be a hundred miles away. We need to find her as soon as possible," Scott said.

"And how are we supposed to do that, exactly?" Stephanie asked.

"We'll split into teams and take separate routes. Levi can go on foot to track her scent. I'll follow in the van and head northeast, where we found the last traces of her trail. I was hoping that one of you could take the pickup and go straight to Gray Mountain, in case Bekah takes a train or some other mode of transportation."

Abel spoke up. "What about us?"

"You and Rylie will stay here with Tyas."

"The hell we will!"

Scott gave him a hard look. "We'll talk about this later." He faced the witches. "Well? Can any of you do it?"

"Travel to Gray Mountain in pursuit of a werewolf?" Blackbird asked uneasily. "Even for Bekah... I don't know, Scott. It could take her two months to walk cross-country as a human. That's four moons. It's a long time to be away from life."

"We'll find her before she makes it across the country," Scott said.

"I'll go," Stephanie said. "There are enough doctors at the clinic to cover me, and if we're releasing a small pack of flesh-hungry teenagers on the country, you might need my medical skills."

His brow furrowed. "Are you sure, Steph? You've barely settled into the job."

"Which means it will be easy for me to leave again."

"You know best. Thank you. I appreciate the help."

Thistle was still trembling. "I have to agree with Blackbird. I'm sorry. Why don't I stay at the sanctuary in case Bekah finds her way back?"

"Great, perfect, whatever," Levi said. "*Great* plan. Really great. So why are we sitting here? We need to go."

Scott rolled up the map. "You're right. There's no time to waste."

Everyone stood, and the meeting was over.

Stephanie departed first, and Scott left with Levi an hour later. Rylie watched them load the van from her bedroom window. She was nauseated by nerves, but she wasn't sure why. It wasn't like she was going with them to the mountain.

The van passed the gates with Levi loping in its wake, like a giant dog chasing cars.

Rylie sat on the bed and stared at one of the paintings Bekah had left behind. She had depicted Gray Mountain perfectly, from the way the line of trees ended a short distance from the highest peaks, down to the warm golden waters of the lake. If she closed her eyes, she could see the wind-whipped pillars at the very top and remember the sting of ice under her paws.

Another motor sounded outside. Probably Thistle going home to pick up a few things for her stay at the sanctuary.

As soon as it was gone, Rylie's door opened. Abel stood on the other side with a duffel bag over his shoulder. "Ready to go?" he asked. He was dressed in a black t-shirt and jeans with heavy hiking boots.

"Huh?"

He tossed the bag onto her floor. It was unzipped, so she could see it was only half-filled with clothes and a few guns with trigger locks. "I saved room for you. Throw some stuff in and let's get out of here." When she didn't immediately move, he huffed. "What, you think we're going to sit here while everyone else goes to Gray Mountain? After all the visions we've been having?"

Rylie frowned. "You didn't mention having the dreams before."

"That's because I'm not a moronic 'let's share our dreams' kind of person. I know a message when I see one. We have to go there."

"No way," she said. "I can't leave this room. What if I change?"

"Then you change. Big deal."

She shook her head. "Scott wants us to stay, and they don't need us to search for Bekah anyway. Nobody will find her faster than Levi."

"I don't care about Bekah. We're going straight to the mountain," Abel said.

As much as she tried not to, she could feel herself nodding along with him. It was like she wasn't in control of her own body. But she hadn't been dreaming about Gray Mountain's gloomy forest for nothing. It wanted her to come back. The idea scared her as much as the idea of being free again.

He crouched in front of her so they were on eye-level, resting his elbows on his knees. "Look, I've been a werewolf hunter for a lot longer than I've been a werewolf. I'm not a fan of letting you out, either. But I won't let you kill anyone."

Rylie bit her lip. "Promise?"

"Yeah. I promise." His big gold eyes were open and honest for once. The scars on his face were healing, but it was still a chilling reminder of what kind of damage she could cause if she went wild.

"If I did change, would you shoot me?"

He laughed. "I did it before."

"I'm serious. If I get out of control, will you shoot me?" She caught his gaze and held it. Abel seemed to understand. He stopped smiling.

"Seth wouldn't forgive me if I killed you. Not ever."

"Forget about Seth. I'm not going anywhere unless you promise."

Slowly, he nodded.

"I promise," Abel said.

Those two words hung in the air between them. Rylie thought the wolf would grow agitated at the threat of death, but it didn't. Instead, as soon as she decided to go back to Camp Silver Brook, it grew eerily calm. "Okay, we can go," she reluctantly agreed. She went to her drawers, but didn't open them. "Give me a minute. Alone."

Abel rolled his eyes and left to wait in the hall.

She packed a few things in the duffel bag. Abel and Seth used to travel a lot with their mom, so he was good at keeping his belongings down to a few essentials. He had one extra pair of jeans, plenty of socks, and a couple of black shirts. Not exactly fashion-forward.

Rylie decided to follow his example and pack the same way. After some internal debate, she changed into clothes appropriate for the transformation: loose linen shirt and pants, and slippers. It was kind of the uniform for the werewolves at the sanctuary. It wouldn't be warm enough if they made it to the mountain, but she didn't have sweaters anymore. California was too temperate.

Rylie hesitated, then grabbed the box of letters from Seth. She removed the letters, put the gun in the bottom, and then concealed it with the envelopes. The lid wouldn't close after that, so she had to wrap hair ties around it to keep it from springing open.

She stuck it in the side of the duffel bag and threw it over her shoulder. It had to be at least fifty pounds with all the guns and ammunition in it, but it felt like nothing more than a bulky pillow to her. There were a few advantages to being a werewolf. Not a lot, but a few.

Abel was waiting at the end of the hallway. He tossed and caught a key ring in one hand repeatedly, and Rylie recognized it as the keys to the sanctuary's gate.

"Ready?" he asked. She nodded. "Great. Let's take you back to Gray Mountain."

Five

Hunters

Seth waited until midnight, when he knew Gwyneth would be asleep, before leaving the ranch.

They had spent the afternoon packing, but Aunt Gwyn had quickly gotten tired, and they agreed to set out for Gray Mountain in the morning instead of driving through the night. But Seth never planned on taking her with him.

As strong as Gwyn was emotionally, she was weak physically. She couldn't keep up at the ranch, much less on the road, and he was pretty sure she would get lax on taking her medication if they had werewolves as a distraction. And if Rylie discovered that Seth had let Gwyn go on a rescue mission at the expense of her health, she would eat him.

So he waited. Once he was sure she was asleep, he picked the lock on the living room cabinet and listened for hints of motion from Gwyn's bedroom. He managed to open it—which took five seconds, a new record for him—and got his rifle out without making a sound. The ammunition was kept on the highest kitchen shelf. He took as much as he could carry and slipped out the front door.

Seth threw his bag in the backseat, put the Chevelle into neutral, and pushed it down the hill without starting the engine. Gwyn was sleeping with her window open.

He turned the car on at the bottom of the hill, but he paused before leaving to take a last look at what had been his home for the past four months. Gazing at the dark ranch filled him with a strange kind of weight. He had never felt so welcome or so happy anywhere else. The Gresham ranch was the closest thing to home he had ever known.

Gwyn would probably have sold it by the time he found Rylie. He was never going to see it again.

With that gloomy thought, he flicked on the headlights and tore down the highway.

Seth left the windows rolled down as he drove. Going fifty-five miles an hour in the middle of the night was a little chilly, but it felt good, and it kept him awake. The road was a black blur speeding underneath him. It felt like he was flying over the pavement.

The weight in his stomach grew as he got into town and parked by the motel.

His mother's black SUV was joined by a twin. They had license plates within one digit of each other, and bumper stickers that said "Union of Kopides and Aspides." So they weren't afraid of advertising themselves. Seth wasn't sure what he thought of that. The existence of the supernatural wasn't common knowledge, especially around those parts.

He checked his reflection in the rearview mirror. Tanned skin. Straight hair. Leather jacket. Haunted, miserable expression. Lying to his mom wouldn't be easy.

Something tapped against his door.

A man stood outside with a shotgun. Seth barely glimpsed it before a flashlight was shined into his eyes. "Identify yourself," said the newcomer.

Seth slowly raised his hands over his shoulders. "I'm Eleanor's son."

"We heard you weren't coming."

"I changed my mind."

"All right. Get out of the car. No sudden motions."

Seth stepped out. The man he faced was shorter than him, and stocky. His shoulders were so broad that it looked like he would have a hard time getting through doorways. "Eleanor's probably expecting me," Seth said cautiously.

To his surprise, the man laughed, put the flashlight away, and gave him a hard clap on the back. "Glad to have you! Didn't mean to scare you, but we've got to be careful these days. Name's Yasir. I'm Union Unit B9's commander."

They shook hands. Yasir had a strong grip and rough palms.

"Commander, huh?"

"Yeah, yeah, what can I say? I left the Marines to escape the machine, and look what I'm doing now."

"Does that mean you're like me?"

"Are you a kopis? Then yeah. We all are, aside from the witches. And your mother, obviously." He leaned in close and lowered his voice. "But between you and me, she's a different kind of witch."

Seth actually laughed. But then he remembered that Yasir was only there because he was hunting werewolves, and his laughter quickly faded.

Yasir led him to room six. All the lights were on inside, and he rapped on the door three times before opening it. Seth had to step over power cords running from the adjacent room to get inside. They had been taped to the threshold, but the bulge was a serious tripping hazard.

The Union had converted the motel room into a small mobile base. They had two laptops with three external monitors set up by the TV. Guns and melee weapons were set out in rows on one of the beds. They had a baton, a machete, and a pickaxe. The blades looked like they might have been dipped in silver.

Two other men stood in the back by the sink, quietly conversing. They fell silent when Seth walked in.

His mother was at the keyboard closest to the door. He didn't think Eleanor even knew how to use a computer. She looked up when he entered, and even though she didn't smile, there was a look of approval in her eyes. "You said you weren't coming."

"Gwyneth Gresham was listening," Seth said with a shrug. "I said what I had to say."

"And Rylie?"

He made himself look away from the silver machete. "We have to stop the werewolves. Whatever it takes."

Eleanor nodded her praise.

"We leave at dawn," she said.

The Union members slept for a few hours on the floor. Seth wasn't tired, so he stood outside the door to enjoy the warm spring air. It hadn't been getting frosty at night. He didn't even need to wear a jacket.

Seth was going to miss that town. He knew everyone who lived in the houses down the road. That old guy who liked to be called Phyllis owned the place with the tin roof. Jean had all the Chihuahuas and the garden with the begonias. Robert, widely regarded as the town bum who drank too much of his stock at the liquor shop, liked to collect ceramic owls.

As weird as they were, each of them always had a friendly word for Seth if they caught him walking after school. Folks appreciated what he did at the Gresham ranch. He felt comfortable and safe there. Like he could really be happy, if only Rylie and Abel would come back.

As if summoned by his contented thoughts, Eleanor joined him in front of the door. "You ought to be sleeping," she said.

"I will. Soon." He nodded at the bumper stickers on the SUV. "So what's up with this Union thing?"

"You might not have noticed while you were doing your very best to hide, but hunters are a dying breed. There used to be whole *legions* of men like you and your daddy. And now there's just handfuls. Hell is winning, boy."

He thought of warm days working Gwyn's ranch and the smell of Rylie's hair. "Yeah. I've noticed," he said dully.

"Hunters are the last line of defense against evil before mankind falls. We've got to regroup. Take back what's ours. The Union's organizing and funding it."

"Where does the money come from?"

"That's none of your business," Eleanor said. "You should enlist. Once we're done exterminating the werewolves, they'll train you and match you up with a good team. The Union can give you the direction that you sorely need."

Seth couldn't resist. "I've got direction, Mom." He clenched and unclenched his fists, trying to suppress the surge of anger. "I guess I'll go to sleep now."

Before he could leave, his mother grabbed his chin in her crushing grip. Her fingernails dug into his jaw. Her lips were twisted with anger. "You think I'm stupid? I haven't forgotten your teenage rebellion. Why the change of heart?"

"My heart hasn't changed at all," he ground out through gritted teeth. "I still hate you."

Her entire body shook. "You little—"

"But this is unfinished business. I have to take care of it."

"Finish it how?" she asked, eyes narrowed. "Finish your daddy's legacy? Or do you have something else in mind?"

He shoved his mom's arm away from him and rubbed drops of blood off of his chin. "I want to be a family again. Okay?"

The sentiment wasn't enough to soften her.

"Good night, Seth. I'll be watching you," Eleanor hissed.

He slept in the backseat of the Chevelle with the doors locked. He didn't trust his mother not to stab him in the middle of the night.

Six

Cheeseburgers

Abel drove through the night. Rylie curled up in the backseat with her head pillowed on the duffel bag and watched orange bars of light slide past the sedan's roof. Her mom would have freaked out if she had seen her daughter in a car without a seat belt, but there didn't seem to be any point in buckling up. She could probably heal from a massive car wreck. And she didn't really care if she couldn't.

They had agreed to drive without stopping until they reached Gray Mountain. That meant they would take shifts behind the wheel, and she needed to sleep when it wasn't her turn. But Rylie couldn't get comfortable.

She could already imagine the smell of icy mountain air, lush with pine and soil and the animals in the forest. She could feel the breeze on her skin. She remembered splashing water from the brook on her face, letting it run through her fingers, and the way the sand sparkled under the surface.

But mostly, she remembered the pain and the fear.

I can't go back.

Denying it didn't make any difference. Abel kept driving. Mile by mile, the mountain drew nearer.

Eventually, the road noises and the motion of the car lulled her to sleep. It wasn't restful. Trees and swollen moons and dead bodies flashed through her mind. She dreamed of crouching over Louise, a counselor who had been kind to her, and ripping out her throat. Rylie knew the taste of human blood on her tongue too well. She didn't have to imagine what it felt like to kill.

She woke up three hours later with dry eyes, a sticky tongue, and a raging headache.

They had already left the state and were deep in the brown monotony of the desert. All she could see in every direction was dirt, dirt, and more dirt. Even the sagebrush struggled to survive.

"Is it my turn?" she asked, sitting up to see Abel over the back of the seat.

He had one finger on the steering wheel and an open bag of beef jerky in his lap. He gnawed on a hunk of dried meat that could have been half of a small cow. "Nah. I'm good."

Rylie rubbed the sleep out of her eyes and stretched. Abel watched her in the rearview mirror.

"What? Is something on my face?"

He swallowed before speaking. "You were making noise in your sleep. Who's Louise?"

Her cheeks flamed with heat. Oh God. At least she hadn't been dreaming about Seth.

"It doesn't matter," she said, climbing into the front seat. She had to push a bunch of open wrappers onto the floor to make a clear spot. Just six hours after setting out, Abel had already made the car a disaster. "I need to use the bathroom."

"Too bad. There are no towns for thirty miles."

"Really? Where are we?"

Abel squinted at the empty desert. "I'm guessing... nowhere. Check the map."

He pointed to a crumpled paper on the dashboard. She smoothed it out on her lap. It was an actual map, with longitude and latitude and dots indicating cities. He had been crossing out towns as they passed and writing timestamps next to landmarks.

"What am I supposed to do with this?" she asked. "There's no way to tell where we are. I mean, we could be anywhere between here…" She stabbed their starting point in California. "And here." She pointed at their destination.

"Are you kidding?"

"Forget it, let me grab my phone. I have GPS."

"Don't use that crap," Abel said as she searched the duffel bag's pockets for her phone. "You can't tell me you don't know how to use a map."

"It's archaic. I'm not a caveman." She tried to turn on her cell phone, but it was dead. "Oh, no! I forgot my car charger!"

"Looks like you'll have to use caveman technology," he said.

She stuck her tongue out at him.

When they finally reached "town," which turned out to be a gas station and a couple of trailers, Abel bought more jerky, a giant hot dog, and boiled eggs. "Your turn to drive," he announced, flopping in the back of the car.

When they got moving again, he was asleep in thirty seconds.

It left Rylie with nothing to do but stare at the empty road. The desert stretched endlessly around them. They couldn't get any radio stations in the middle of nowhere, so the only music available was a cassette tape of Santana's greatest hits. Rylie enjoyed listening to it for a few minutes, but when it cut off with a grinding noise, she didn't know how to start the tape over again.

So she drove in silence, alone with her thoughts.

It wasn't a pleasant place to be. After months of trying to suppress her memories of the massacre at Camp Silver Brook, all it took was one bad dream to bring it back. Louise hadn't been the only one who had died at camp. Amber had been the first to go. Rylie had seen her body, and she could remember the ragged shreds of her throat and bloodstained hands. She had gone out trying to protect herself, and failed. Humans didn't stand a chance against werewolves.

None of the humans that Rylie had killed back home had fought against her. She had attacked too fast.

Trying to push away those thoughts, she focused on the rippling heat lines on the horizon instead. The sun was climbing fast. It was getting hot. She punched the air conditioning button and sighed at the chilly air.

After a couple of hours, bushes started to appear, and then trees, and signs of human life followed. Abel woke up when Rylie parked in front of the first fast food place she saw.

"What's going on?" he asked, instantly alert.

"I'm hungry."

"So eat some jerky. We're not stopping for lunch."

She turned off the car. "I can't drive forever. It's boring. I want to walk around." Rylie stepped out with the keys, leaving him with no choice but to follow her.

It looked like the restaurant might have been the only burger joint in town, and they had hit the lunch rush. The line to order was all the way out the door. Rylie took position at the back. Abel lurked at her side, grumpy and puffy-faced from sleep. "It's going to take forever to get across the country if you want to stop every few minutes."

"You were asleep for five hours."

"Really?" He looked a tiny bit mollified. "I can take the next leg. And we're driving until the tank runs dry. You got it?"

She rolled her eyes. "Fine."

There was a time when Rylie had been scared of Abel. He towered over her head and shoulders, and all the death threats were pretty unsettling. But things had changed. Hanging out for four months and seeing all his dumb quirks—like the fact that he enjoyed John Hughes movies—shifted the balance of power a lot. It helped that she could kick his butt as a werewolf, too.

That didn't stop everyone from staring as they entered the restaurant. Abel towered over her head and shoulders, and his scars were pretty conspicuous.

The tables inside were completely full, but someone left just as they got in. "I'll get a table," Rylie said. "Order a bunch of cheeseburgers, okay?"

He threw an ironic salute at her. "Of course, your majesty."

She hurried to the table before anyone else could take it, and stretched her legs out on the seat across from her. Changing positions after hours in a car was nice, even if the hard benches weren't comfortable.

Someone approached the table. "Are you okay?"

Rylie tensed before she looked up. It was an old lady with a white perm. She relaxed a fraction of an inch. "What?"

"I saw you come in with that man and wanted to make sure nothing was wrong." She kept her voice in a low whisper, as if worried that Abel would hear her over the clamor of voices in the burger place. Her eyes were narrow. Calculating. Trying to decide if a petite blond girl was really with someone as intimidating as Abel.

It probably shouldn't have been funny, but Rylie had to laugh anyway. She was a hundred times more dangerous than Abel. "Don't worry about me."

"Are you sure you're okay, dear?" the old lady pressed.

Was she okay? No. Not at all. And she wasn't safe with Abel, either, but that was beside the point. Rylie plastered on her most innocent smile. "I'm fine. Thank you so much."

Obviously, that wasn't the right answer. The woman gave her a disapproving look and walked away.

Abel dropped the receipt on the table. "We're number seventy. Who was that?"

"She wanted to know if you kidnapped me."

Any hint of mirth in his eyes was gone immediately. He glared at the woman, who had sat down with a group of other people her age. They were whispering amongst themselves. "What did you tell her?"

"I told her you're a hairy monster who's feeding me a last meal before my horrible, gruesome death. What do you think?"

"Stupid old cow," he muttered.

Having people stare and whisper at Abel threw him into a sullen silence for the next several minutes, leaving Rylie with nothing to do but shred a napkin into progressively tinier pieces. It took almost twenty minutes for their number to get called. Abel slouched low on the bench, and she had to climb over his legs to get the tray.

He must have spent half their cash on cheeseburgers. There were over a dozen. But they smelled too good for her to complain, so Rylie ripped one open and ate it on the way back to the table. "We'll put this place out of business," she said, starting on her second burger.

Abel removed the buns from three of the cheeseburgers and stacked the patties together. "Good. So who's Louise?"

Rylie wadded up one of the wrappers and chucked it into the trash. "She was a counselor at Camp Silver Brook." She wiped some of the ketchup off a burger before taking a big, cheesy bite.

"If you're having nightmares about her, I'm betting she's dead."

"Yeah. Louise is dead." The hamburger was a thick lump in her throat. "She was nice to me."

He finished his three patties and opened another one. "You know, whatever's calling us to the mountain won't be good. *Werewolves* aren't good. I bet this is some super Alpha werewolf monster thing."

"Have you seen a super Alpha werewolf monster thing before?"

"Naw. But that doesn't mean they don't exist. I've seen Alphas collect packs of werewolves, and they're always the meanest, the hungriest, and the most vicious. Hunters don't stand a chance against them." He laughed bitterly. "Guess it's a good thing I'm not on the human team anymore."

"Maybe it's not anything like that," Rylie said. "Maybe we're just getting called home."

He snorted. "Home?"

She shrugged, poking at a pickle she had dropped onto the table. "I don't know."

The bell over the door, and two more people stepped into line. A strange smell caught her attention as the line of people standing by the door shifted. It set every alarm bell in her head ringing before she could even process what the odor meant.

It was woody and earthy with an underlying musk. It smelled like wolf.

Rylie went still. "Do you smell that?"

Abel's eyes were already scanning the people standing in line. His golden eyes narrowed. "Werewolves," he muttered.

That made the restaurant about two people too crowded for Rylie. She swallowed the last burger, balled up her trash, and threw it all out.

They're in my territory.

The thought rose to the surface above everything else, even though she knew it was stupid. Some burger joint in Idaho was hardly *her* territory.

But there was no talking reason with her inner wolf. It swelled and grew, and her fingernails began to itch. "Let's get out of here," she said, grabbing a fistful of napkins. The words came out slurred and thick. Her teeth were loosening.

He saw her hand and grabbed her wrist. "Stop it. Not here."

The pinch of his grip only aggravated the wolf. "It's not my choice. Let me go!"

Abel ignored her and steered them out the back, which led onto a patio. The wind was picking up as clouds moved over the sun, so there weren't as many people dining outside. Only one table was occupied, and when they saw Abel's massive form lumber through the doorway, they finished very quickly.

Rylie grabbed the fence with both hands, trying to ground herself in reality despite the wolf's growing fury. She shut her eyes to focus. She wanted to feel the wind in her face and the metal bar in her hands. There was a cell phone in her pocket and a headband holding her blond hair—*human* hair—out of her face.

Human things. Not wolf things.

They're in my territory. Fight them. Kill them.

Abel's deep voice rose behind her.

"What are you doing?"

It took her a moment to realize he wasn't speaking to her. She took a slow, deep breath, and turned around.

His broad back shielded her from the newcomers, but she could smell the wolves again. The responding voice had a Canadian accent. "We don't want a fight. We smelled you and wanted to see what's up."

Rylie peered around Abel's shoulder. The speaker was thin and scruffy with a graying beard. His companion was a short woman with a pixie cut and overalls. Their dirty clothing didn't fit right, like they had fished it out of a trashcan.

"You're werewolves," Abel said. One of his hands reached back, and Rylie realized he was moving for his gun.

A fight.

Rylie grabbed the fence again and took deep breaths.

"We're only passing through," said the woman. She paused, and then added, "We don't have to fight for territory... right?"

Abel's low growl clearly meant he was wondering the same thing. "Where are you going?"

"The same place you are, I bet," said the man. "We thought we were the only ones heading to the big mountain by the lake until we came across another one of us doing the same thing."

"Have you seen many others?"

It was the woman who responded. "We just ran across the one guy in Boise."

"So you haven't seen a kid wandering around?" Abel asked. "Curly hair, about this tall... She can go wolf whenever she wants, so she might not look human. Kinda light brown fur?"

"She can turn at will?" asked the man, his voice sharpening. "No way."

The wind shifted and blew the smell of the two other werewolves at Rylie. Her whole jaw ached as her teeth loosened.

They're in my territory.

"Shut up," she whispered to herself, quietly enough that nobody else would hear.

"She's just a kid," Abel said. "Her name's Bekah. Rebekah Riese. If you see her, tell her that her dad is trying to find her."

"We'll do that," said the woman. "Guess we'll see you on the mountain."

Rylie didn't hear their footsteps, but she felt them move away. They slipped into the forest beyond the road.

Her pulse pounded in her temples, and she still felt dizzyingly close to transformation, but it got easier to hang on to her human body as they got farther away. When their scent was nothing but a stale odor on the breeze, she opened her eyes and spread her hands in front of her. She had only lost two fingernails this time. They would grow back in a minute. They always did.

Abel waited nearby. "Are you human?" he asked when she turned around. She nodded. "Get in the car. We're going."

Seven

Yasir

Yasir talked constantly while they were on the road. He had a lot of weird, discomfiting stories that were also somehow entertaining.

Seth learned three important things from the older hunter as they followed the short convoy of black SUVs: first, that Yasir had killed a lot of people in the Marines, and he wasn't very sorry about it; second, that the Union made him commander specifically for that reason; and finally, that the Union was turning that ruthlessness toward hunting a specific group of werewolves.

"We've been following this guy for the last five days," he explained, typing rapidly on a laptop in the passenger's seat of the Chevelle. "I'm waiting for him to hook up with other wolves before we hit him, but we want to catch their cluster before they reach the mountain. We pinned one of them with a tracker back in Vancouver. See?"

He swiveled his screen around so Seth could glance at it while he drove. A squiggly blue line traced a long route from Canada down through Washington, and then into Idaho.

The Union must have made a pretty big detour to visit Seth. He wasn't sure how he felt about his mom going so far out of her way to ruin his life.

"What are you going to do when you catch the werewolves?" he asked.

Yasir looked surprised. "Kill them. What did you expect?"

"I thought Union command might have other plans."

"Ah, well." He returned his attention to the laptop. "There are rules about what we do. We have to verify lycanthropy before the kill, ideally with a visual confirmation. And we collect teeth or skins to keep them counted."

"That's what my dad did, too," Seth said.

Yasir took a couple books out of his bag. The top one was a new edition of "The Legends of Gray Mountain," but the second one was tattered and yellowing. Seth didn't have to look at the cover to know what the title was, or who the author would be. His stomach gave a funny flop when he saw it.

"Your dad did write the book on werewolf hunting." Yasir flapped the pages in the air. "The Union used it to develop regulations."

"So we can't kill them until the next moon anyway."

The commander typed faster. "There are ways to make a wolf turn before the moon hits." Yasir's tone suddenly changed. "Take the next exit." He thumbed a device in his ear. "Hear me? Take the next exit."

Seth glanced at the laptop screen. The blue line was flashing.

"What's going on?"

"He stopped. We're going to check on him," Yasir said.

They exited by a small town that was populated with a gas station and three houses, and then passed it. The farther they got from the freeway, the bumpier the road became. It lost the lines halfway across a field of cattle. Yasir told the convoy to stop.

The entire team got out. One of the other men, who went by the name "Stripes" for no reason Seth could see, tossed a sniper rifle to Yasir.

"What are we doing?" Seth asked as the commander handed the gun to him and took another.

"Can you shoot?"

"Yeah, I'm a pretty good shot. Why?"

"You can come with me. You all stay with the vehicles to provide support." He tapped his earpiece. Seth felt Eleanor's eyes follow him as he climbed over the fence into the field. Yasir led him to the edge, which was on the side of a hill overlooking more farms. "So tell me, Seth, son of Eleanor— you just graduated from high school, right? What do you want to do with yourself?"

"I want to go to medical school."

"Doctor, huh? Noble. Where are you going to college?"

It was too embarrassing to admit the truth. "I haven't decided."

The commander cut the barbed wire fence with clippers and let Seth through to the other side. He slid a short distance down the hill, found a flat spot behind a boulder, and stopped. He propped his elbows on the rock to scan the farms below with binoculars.

He spoke into his earpiece. "Is he still there?" Seth couldn't hear the response, but Yasir seemed satisfied by whatever they said. "You know what, kid? I like you. You remind me of myself before I went into the Marines."

It took Seth a moment to realize Yasir wasn't speaking to the team anymore. He wasn't sure what to say. Fortunately, the commander didn't seem to expect a response, and kept talking.

"My dad's gone, too. My surviving family is on the other side of the world. And my mom was a terrible—really terrible—person before she died." He propped the sniper rifle on the boulder, and gestured for Seth to do the same. "But you're a good guy. I can tell. You've got a lot of heart. Maybe too much." He peered through the eyepiece. "Life's a lot easier if you learn to let go, like I did during my tours of duty. Look behind the farm."

SM Reine

Seth did as instructed. It took him a few seconds of tracking the scope along the fence to reach the farm, and when he did, it took him another few seconds to find the people waiting around it.

"Are those farmers?"

"Look at the way they move," Yasir said. "Tell me if they're farmers. Take your time."

He watched the group walk. There were two women and one man. He paced and waved his hands in the air, and his head twitched occasionally, like there were flies buzzing around his face that he couldn't swat. One of the women glared at him. The other didn't look at her companions at all.

At first, they looked like ordinary people. Angry, but normal. But Seth had learned a few things when he hunted werewolves as a child. The one on the ground wasn't ignoring the others; she was watching their surroundings, fearful of being discovered. The man looked like he had psychosis, which was common in late-stage lycanthropy. And the standing woman looked every inch the predator.

Seth couldn't make out their irises, even with telescopic vision, but he had seen enough werewolves to know them on sight. A lead weight settled in his gut.

"Those aren't farmers," he said, voice hoarse.

"Like I said, Seth, you're a good guy. So that's why I want you to help me on this one." Yasir rested a hand on Seth's shoulder. It was heavy enough to force him to lower his upper chest to the rock. "Listen to me: take a deep breath and let it out. Keep your sights steady. Then shoot the standing woman."

Seth couldn't breathe, much less fire. "But they're human."

"I told you, there's more than one way to make a wolf change. Look at this." He ejected the cartridge from his gun and showed one of the rounds to Seth. The tip was silver. "This is a soft alloy that pulverizes on impact. It will hurt to get hit, but they won't die." He jammed it back into the rifle. "One of the better Union inventions, if you ask me."

The intent was painfully clear: Yasir wanted to give them silver poisoning. It was the fastest, easiest way to make a werewolf lose its mind. Given enough time, they would start changing uncontrollably between moons, although that group already looked stressed enough to be on the edge of snapping.

"So we shoot them," Seth said slowly, "and then they change in a couple of days so we can identify and kill them."

Yasir looked pleased that he had caught on. "Go ahead."

Seth put his eye to the scope again and relocated the standing woman. She didn't resemble Rylie at all. His girlfriend was skinny and blond. The woman was broad-shouldered, tall, and muscular. She was probably at least his mom's age.

But when he looked at her, all he could see was Rylie.

"You shoot her, I will shoot the man, and then I'll pick off the one on the ground before she can run," Yasir said in a low voice behind his ear. "Three easy shots."

A year before, Seth wouldn't have cared about firing. He had killed werewolves. Inflicting silver poisoning wouldn't be the worst thing he had done to score a kill. But that had been when he thought that werewolves lost their soul after the bite. Before he knew the truth.

Did the people down there have brothers and girlfriends, too?

But if he didn't shoot, the Union would know he was up to something. And knowing Eleanor, he would get tied up somewhere. He didn't know how he could reach Rylie and Abel without maintaining the ruse.

The woman walked a few steps. Seth kept his sights on her.

"On the count of three," Yasir said, getting into position.

What were three strangers' lives in comparison to Rylie's?

"One... two..."

Seth's finger tightened on the trigger.

"Three."

Eight

Midnight

Rylie dreamed of Gray Mountain again. She dreamed of its frozen peak, the tangled forest, and the dead people on the shore of the lake.

When she woke up the next morning, they were two states away from where she had fallen asleep, and they were in the middle of rolling hills. Abel decided they should take a short break at a rest stop bathroom. She agreed.

Rylie took the gun with her.

She locked herself in a stall, eased the weapon from the box, and hefted its weight in her hands. She chewed on her bottom lip.

The gun wasn't heavy. She could probably bench press a car if she wanted to (which she didn't), so a pistol definitely wasn't a problem. But it made her *feel* heavy to look at it, to rub her fingers over the mechanisms, to open it up and pull out the silver bullet again.

The sting of silver on her skin and in her nose was a welcome burn. It hurt, but not the way that losing her fingernails hurt, or the way that spitting human teeth onto the ground like falling stars hurt. It was a pain she could control. In fact, the gun gave her a lot of control—the choice to never change again.

What if she had turned into a werewolf at the burger joint? There must have been more than fifty people crammed in the restaurant with their families. She imagined the faces of smiling children and happy parents, and she thought of killing them. Leaving behind nothing but blood.

Rylie couldn't do it again. She just couldn't.

The gun gave her a choice.

She slipped her finger over the trigger and wondered where she should aim. Rylie had been shot before. She wasn't scared of how it would feel. She was only scared that she would survive it.

A fist pounded on the door to the bathroom. "Rylie!" Abel shouted. He sounded annoyed.

She considered her choices: doing it right that moment so she wouldn't have to get back in the car traveling to Gray Mountain, or putting the gun away and hoping she could transform again without hurting anyone. Her breath was stuck in her chest.

Did she *really* want to do it?

He knocked again.

"You're taking forever," he said with a note of teasing in his voice. "Did you fall in?"

"Leave me alone!" Rylie yelled back.

She took Seth's letters out of the box, put the gun in the bottom, and covered it again. Her cheeks burned. Her heart was beating too fast.

"Come *on*, we still have at least another day of driving."

She went outside. Abel had his fist raised to knock again, but he stopped when she emerged. He looked half-irritated and half-suspicious. "Can't I use the bathroom alone?" she snapped.

"What's the problem? All those burgers getting to you?"

Her cheeks flushed. "You're gross."

Abel laughed. Then his eyes fell on the box, and his amusement vanished. She thought he might have looked sympathetic for an instant before he reassumed his bored, I-don't-care-about-anything look, but she also might have imagined it.

When he spoke again, he was more serious. "I did some looking around. I have something to show you."

He led her to the edge of the rest stop, which was separated from an empty field by a span of gravel. Abel tilted his head back to sniff the air, and Rylie followed suit. The faint odor of werewolves made her hackles rise.

They paced the gravel for a few minutes as she drank in the smells. The pheromones were telling. There had been three of them: a middle-aged man and two young women. They were sweating a lot, and they smelled sick. Following the odor to the fence, Rylie crouched down. Vomit dried next to one of the posts. "What do you think?" Abel asked. "Two of them?"

"Three," she said. What was making them sick?

"So it's not the same people we saw at the restaurant."

She shook her head. "How big is this thing?" she asked, hugging the closed box of letters to her chest. "We've already come across five of them. That's a lot of werewolves."

"Only one way to find out," Abel said. "It's your turn to drive, by the way."

Rylie put the box on the floor of the car. Her hands lingered on the lid for a moment as she contemplated the gun one more time. It made her feel better to know that the choice was waiting for her, even if she hadn't made the decision yet.

But she would soon. Very soon.

She got back on the freeway.

•○•

Time didn't make very much sense on the road. Cars and towns blurred past them. They stopped and started and slept fitfully and ate gas station food. Farms turned to cities, and then became farms again, which turned to forest.

Rylie woke up disoriented the next night, and it took her an entire minute to realize she had woken up at all. At first, she thought she was still dreaming about Gray Mountain, but then she realized that she was resting on leather seats. It was completely dark aside from the yellow-green glow of dashboard lights, which projected Abel's shadow on the roof of the car.

They weren't moving anymore.

"Are we there?" she asked, sitting up with a small groan. Even werewolf healing couldn't do anything for the stiffness in her muscles.

Abel didn't respond. His fists were clenched on the steering wheel.

She cleared her throat and tried again.

"Are we there?"

"Shh," he said.

She peered out the window. She could make out the trunks of towering trees and smell pine through the car vents. It looked familiar. They must have been getting close. So why had they stopped?

Rylie climbed into the front seat.

"Don't move," Abel whispered. "We're not alone."

She followed his gaze and noticed a group of murky shapes a few feet away. Rylie leaned toward the vent and took a deeper sniff, closing her eyes to savor the subtle odors. Distant ice water, soil, rotting plants. But there was also the musk of fur and feces.

The shapes were a herd of deer. They didn't seem to have noticed the car.

"I don't think they'll attack us," Rylie whispered back.

He shook his head. "There are werewolves out there."

"In wolf form?" she asked. He nodded. "That's not possible. It isn't a moon."

Then she saw it—a flash of fur.

Even a glimpse of it was enough to stir the wolf inside of her. Rylie was still groggy and half-asleep, but her wolf wasn't, and it responded to the sight of another werewolf too fast for her to fight back. Her ribs creaked as it swelled inside of her.

She grunted, wrapped her arms around herself, and bowed her head to her knees.

Abel didn't seem to notice. He was too transfixed by the deer.

Her shoulders twitched. Her spine ached. Rylie focused with all her strength on human things, like Seth had told her to do, but looking at the speedometer and her shoes and the seams of the leather seats wasn't enough this time. Not when she could smell those deer. She was so hungry, and now that she had seen them, they were *her* deer—but that wolf was already out there, already on the hunt, and it was going to get them before she could if she didn't move fast—

One of her cheekbones popped.

The sound caught Abel's attention. "Not right now," he hissed. She whimpered as her mouth flooded with blood and her teeth fell onto her tongue. "Rylie, this is not the time. Get a grip."

Taking long, shallow breaths, she silently counted to fifty. When she got to ten, her fingernails had loosened again, and by the time she got to thirteen, the claws began to emerge. Her tailbone snapped. Her back arched, and she gripped her face in bleeding hands. *Nineteen, twenty, twenty-one… get a grip, Rylie!*

The numbers weren't calming her. Focusing on human things wasn't calming her. And when the wind shifted to bring the smell of four wolves outside the car to her through the vent, that definitely didn't help.

Abel grabbed her wrists. "Stop it!"

"I can't," she whimpered.

A clump of hair loosened from her head and slithered to the floor. Her scalp itched as fur emerged in its place.

Panic filled Abel's eyes. He shoved her back against the seat, using his weight to hold her down. "I don't want to shoot you," he said with none of his usual bravado.

Abel was interrupted by an explosion of motion outside the car, even more violent than Rylie's motions within.

The werewolves attacked the deer. They fell on the herd like a storm of teeth and claws. The deer tried to run, but they weren't fast enough. Nothing would have been fast enough to escape the fury of a werewolf pack.

It turned out that deer could actually scream.

The sound of death was enough for Rylie to blink out of her own skull, like flicking a light switch, and the wolf took her place.

Calm spread through her and pushed away the pain. The wolf sniffed at the human that had it pinned back against the bench seat of the Chevelle. His body was strangely bald, and those were hands on her legs instead of the proper paws, but it was her pack. He was not her enemy.

The wolves outside, on the other hand—those smells were completely new. And they smelled sick. Their growls and yips as they tore into the deer were too savage, even for werewolves.

She thrashed underneath Abel's weight, trying to free herself so she could confront them.

"Stop moving!"

She ripped a paw free—her body was all wolf now—and shoved. His back struck the driver's side door.

Abel reached for her again. She snapped, and her teeth sunk into flesh. He cried out.

Satisfied that he knew who was in control again, she turned her attention to more important things.

The wolf slammed her body into the glass by her head. It cracked. She did it again, and again.

The windshield shattered and sagged inward. She pushed through it with her head and shoulders, and her paws scrabbled for traction on the dashboard. The safety glass scraped uselessly against her fur. One more hard shove, and she was through.

With all four paws planted on the hood of the sedan, she was taller than the other wolves, and could get a good look at what they had done.

One of the deer had run off, but the rest were not so lucky. The wolves were feasting.

Rylie threw back her head and gave a short howl that echoed through the trees. The feasting wolves froze and turned four pairs of luminous gold eyes toward her just before she leaped at them.

A half-second later, a black SUV burst into the clearing.

Buffalo River Regional Library
Columbia, TN 38401

Nine

Collisions

The Union tracked the werewolves they shot for a couple of days. The silver poisoning took effect as soon as the bullets hit, but it was several hours before the effects got nasty.

First, they fought with each other over the source of the gunshots. One of the women insisted it was an unseen farmer trying to get them off his land; the other said it was an assassin. The man only rambled about paranoid things, mostly the government and mind control.

Second, the paranoia began overtaking the women, too. Their rationality faded. They jogged across the farms with jerky, twitching motions until running got too hard. They lost coordination. The man fell down and couldn't seem to get up again.

Third, they got hungry.

They limped into a field of cows, continuing to argue and twitch and have the occasional seizure. Their bodies hadn't started to change, but the shift in their minds was obvious. They stopped navigating like humans and approached the cows like a wolf pack. They circled around a stray calf. When the cattle fled, they didn't let the calf go with the rest of the herd. And then they fell on it and began to eat.

Seth watched Yasir's monitor with horror as human hands and human teeth ripped into the calf. The werewolves were clearly unaware that they were being watched from a road a half-mile away by two vehicles with enhanced surveillance systems. Although by that point, the Union probably could have walked up to them without being noticed.

Seth thought he might throw up.

When the pack was done, they started arguing again. One woman gesticulated wildly with bloody hands, while the other gripped her stomach as though she was still starving.

The man collapsed on all fours. His spine cracked.

Seth had been given a Union earpiece so he could follow the conversation between vehicles. Stripes hooted as blood sprayed out of the man's face and misted the ground. His jaw and nose elongated.

"Twenty bucks!" he told the other Union team member, who was named Jakob. "Pay up, dude."

"You said it was going to take two days!"

"Look at the time, nimrod. It's been almost three days now."

Only Eleanor was silent, but Seth could see her smiling on the intra-vehicle cameras. He really hated that smile.

"That must be a record," Yasir said, making note of the time on his laptop. The sun was dropping outside as night approached. "I've never seen it take effect that fast."

Seth was so disgusted that he couldn't think of a response.

"That's more than enough verification," Eleanor said with her fingers to her earpiece. "We can end the hunt now."

Yasir closed his laptop lid. "Yeah. We can."

"Leave them for a few minutes," Jakob said. "I want to see how much of the herd they can take out."

"That's against regulations," argued Stripes. "The cattle are someone's private property. We're here to protect humans and take out werewolves, not cost some rancher half his cows."

Seth tightened his hands on the steering wheel of the Chevelle. He didn't want to be there anymore. He didn't want to have to listen to them discuss the fate of people whose only offense had been to get bitten by the wrong animal.

He powered his earpiece off, turned from the monitor, and watched the light fading in the sky.

Yasir kept talking to the rest of the unit. Seth tried not to listen, but when the commander exclaimed over something happening with the herd, he couldn't resist glancing at the monitor again.

The pack had killed an adult cow. Now that the man had a wolf's jaw, he was gulping down massive bites of meat. The weaker of the women started to change, too. She rolled onto her side and sobbed as her body shifted. Her companions kept eating.

The crying was too much, especially since it only made Eleanor's smile widen.

He reached out to turn off the intra-vehicle cameras.

Yasir caught his wrist. "Don't touch that," he said sharply. He hadn't been quite as friendly since Seth failed to shoot any of the wolves with the sniper rifle. One of the women had almost escaped. He knew that Yasir was wondering if his bad aim had been deliberate or not.

"Sorry. My mom..."

The commander watched her for a few moments. His eyes darkened at her gleeful expression, and he turned off his earpiece. "I've seen her type before. The people who really enjoy it." He waved at the monitors. "This seems weird to you, doesn't it? Betting on the lives of werewolves when we should kill them. The men are just blowing off steam. But your mother..."

Yasir hesitated, and then turned the monitor off.

Seth ducked his head. "Thanks."

The commander reengaged his earpiece. His voice hardened. "This is what we're going to do: we'll circle around the field and catch them on the other side. We need to draw them out before there's too much property destruction, so we'll spray some pheromones to get them moving. You two move in to cut them off."

"That won't be necessary," Eleanor said.

"Are you questioning me?"

"No. They're already on the move... sir."

Both Yasir and Seth turned their attention back to the laptop. The telescopic camera mounted on the first SUV was keyed to motion, so it should have tracked the werewolves no matter where they went, but the screen only showed a bunch of bloody ribs that had been gnawed to stubs.

"Find them!" he barked.

The cameras scanned. Seth got out of the car and propped his elbows on the hood as he searched with the binoculars.

He didn't look for the wolves. Instead, he imagined the route they would take, decided how long they had been moving, and made an educated guess about their location. Given the forest stretching beyond the ranch, it wasn't hard to guess where they would go.

Seth spotted them moving into the trees. He tracked their path until their gray tails disappeared into shadow, and a hint of relief eased through him.

It took another twenty seconds for the equipment to pick them up.

Inside the Chevelle, Yasir swore loudly. "They're gone. Damn it! Get in, we've got to move!" Seth jumped into the driver's seat just in time to follow the SUVs as they peeled down the mountain road. "Faster, kid! They're going for the mountain."

"I don't think so," Seth said. "Not yet. They're scared, the mountain is still a few miles away, and they've eaten. They'll find somewhere to den in the forest."

He tried not to smile when he said it. There were a lot of places werewolves could den without being found. The forest became very thick, very fast once they got to the other side of the pass, and that was less than a mile away. They would never catch them in time.

Jakob and Stripes seemed to realize it, because they jumped the SUVs off the road to cut them off.

Seth tried to follow. Abel would have beaten him around the head if he saw his little brother off-roading in his baby, but the Chevelle didn't make it far in the forest anyway. They hit a cluster of brush and got stuck.

Yasir jumped out. "Open the doors!" he shouted to the rear SUV.

It stopped, and he waved to Seth to climb in.

The only seat in the back was next to Eleanor, who was still grinning maniacally. She gripped her husband's book on hunting werewolves in both hands. Her smile faded a fraction when she saw Seth.

The SUV bounced through the forest. He had to grip the handhold to keep from getting thrown out of his seat.

"They're moving fast," Jakob said through the earpiece. "We're a mile behind them."

"Take your vehicle north. Stripes will take us south. Find an opening—we'll get around them." He climbed into the cargo area, pushed away empty gas tanks, and flung open one of the rear doors. A few boxes of supplies fell out, but he didn't seem to care.

Seth's heart thudded in his throat as they chased the werewolves. He watched the tracking monitor through the gap in the front seats, and saw them close in on the blinking blue line.

The flashing dot disappeared. Seth swerved to get around it.

"Closing fast, sir!"

"Seth! Give me the gun!" Yasir shouted.

He hesitated only a moment before passing a rifle over the seat. The commander braced himself against the side of the

SUV, dug his feet in, and took aim at the trees. A deer darted past the back door.

Eleanor grabbed the other rifle and took position next to Yasir.

"Hit the floods!" he ordered.

Seth pressed his face to the side window as the lights cast the forest in a ghastly white glow. The humans had completely wolfed out and left a massacre in their wake. There was blood and meat everywhere. He wouldn't have had any clue they were deer if he hadn't seen the survivor running away.

When the lights hit the werewolves, they plunged into the forest again. Stripes took a hard left to follow.

"There's a car," Jakob reported.

Yasir frowned. "Repeat that."

"There's a car parked in a thicket north of your location. Shattered windshield. No sign of people."

Seth glimpsed it as they drove past in pursuit of the werewolves. It was a silver Ford sedan. There was blood on the hood of the car.

"I'm on their tails," Stripes said. "Turning us around."

The SUV whipped around, cutting off his view of the abandoned car. Seth lost his balance and sprawled against the side door in time to see the pack of werewolves cut off by the other vehicle. All four of them were pinned between the two SUVs.

A cold realization shocked through Seth.

Four wolves? There had only been three people.

Eleanor and Yasir opened fire. Howls filled the air, and yips of pain followed. Something had been hit.

Seth grabbed one of the handguns and wrenched open the side door. He waited until the SUV stopped before jumping out.

"I didn't give you permission to go," Yasir said over the earpiece. "You're in the line of fire!"

"I saw something!"

Curses filled the channel on the earpiece from all the team members. People shouting. More gunshots. Seth turned it off and dove through the trees.

One of the wolves broke free. He saw white-gold fur and a slender body in the floodlights for an instant before she disappeared. Seth recognized that fur. It was almost identical to Rylie's hair, but thicker and shaggier. She was still sleeker than the other werewolves.

"Oh, *no*—"

He chased the wolf, moving away from the rest of the team.

His eyes didn't have time to adjust to the darkness. All he saw was black. He clambered over a fallen log, between trees, over rocks, running mostly on adrenaline and instinct.

His foot splashed in something wet. He paused for an instant—he had found a brook off the main river, and the water was as cold as ice—and then sloshed through. It only went to his ankles.

Starlight shone through a gap in the trees. Gold fur sparkled on a ridge above him as a wolf jumped to the top.

"Rylie!" he shouted.

But she was already gone.

He scrambled up the slope, digging his fingers into the rock and kicking off with his legs. He was strong and fast, but not as strong or as fast as the wolf. By the time he got to the top, there was no hint of her.

But someone else was waiting for him.

Seth's eyes finally adjusted, and he could see the dark shape of a human standing back in the trees. The new person was tall and broad-shouldered.

"Hey, bro," Abel said. He stepped forward. His clothes were torn, he was carrying a gun, and mud was splattered all over him. Seth felt a surge of joy.

"Abel!"

His brother didn't respond with the same smile. He looked angry and confused.

Seth wanted to jump on him and hug him and punch him, but when he looked over his shoulder, he saw approaching floodlights. The Union was looking for a route up the mountain.

"Run," Seth said. "Run! Don't lose her!"

He didn't have to say it again. Abel gave him a salute that was only half-ironic and ran after Rylie.

Seth turned on his earpiece again.

"One of them broke free," he said. "I lost it."

"It's fine. We killed two of them. We've got your position. See you in a minute," Yasir said. He stood on top of the boulders, exposed to the chilly wind, and waited for the SUV to reach him. The commander hauled him into the back. "Do that again, and I'll shoot you," he said without releasing Seth's arm. He smiled when he said it, but the smile didn't reach his eyes. "Understand?"

"I couldn't miss my chance," he said.

The commander caught the double meaning. His hand tightened. "Don't do it again."

Jakob spoke from the other SUV. "There's a girl! A human girl!"

Fear gripped Seth, but he tried not to show it. There wasn't enough time for Rylie to have turned back. It had to be someone else. It *had* to be.

Eleanor's order rang out like a gunshot: "Get her."

She slammed the doors shut and climbed back into the main compartment of the SUV as it peeled off again. Seth followed.

There were two wolf bodies stacked by the side door of the vehicle. The bottom one had brown fur that was almost black. The other was a dirty red color. Even though Seth knew that they had been killed before he had seen Rylie, he was still relieved to see that neither was gold.

"I've got her!" Jakob reported. Seth shut his eyes to pray.

"Convene by my coordinates," Yasir ordered.

Seth didn't breathe until the other SUV joined them. Everyone unloaded.

Eleanor shoved past him to run to Jakob first. Seth elbowed her. She shot a nasty look at him and raced him to the body, but the team was in the way.

"Move it!" Seth said, and Stripes seemed so surprised to hear him yell that he obeyed without questioning. He moved aside, letting Seth see inside the SUV.

But it wasn't Rylie between the seats.

The girl had curls that were long and honey-blond. Her olive skin was dotted with freckles, and smeared with enough blood that he couldn't tell if she was wounded or not. He knew that if she opened her eyes, they would be brown and shot through with gold.

She was only wearing shorts and a t-shirt, so he pulled off his jacket and laid it over her curled body, which was a lot thinner than he remembered.

He had found Bekah Riese. And she was unconscious in the hands of the Union.

Ten

Expert Advice

The Union picked a spot by the brook to camp for the night. They parked the SUVs before addressing the bodies. Stripes broke teeth out of the jaws of the werewolves they had killed, stamped numbers into the bone, and the team buried the bodies. Seth dug one of the graves himself. He whispered a prayer as he dragged the black-furred wolf into the ground.

Once the graves were concealed, they discussed what to do with Bekah.

"Nobody saw her change, so I don't think she's one of the werewolves. I bet she's a camper," Stripes said.

"Nobody asked you what you think. You're not here for what you *think*. It's obviously another wolf converging!" Eleanor said. She had been even more irate since finding Bekah. She had clearly hoped that Jakob would find Rylie.

Her moping was making Seth angrier by the minute. "We have no way of knowing that," he snapped.

She glowered. "Who else would be out here?"

Jakob was cleaning mud from under his fingernails with a knife. He had gotten messy digging graves. "We saw a wrecked car. Bet that's where she came from."

"Do you see any signs of a car wreck on her?" she asked.

Everyone standing around the SUV turned to look at Bekah again. She was asleep between the seats with her wrists and ankles trussed together. Having so many ropes for such a short girl looked ridiculous, but if she tried to break free, it still wouldn't be enough. Each of the kopides studied her like she was on a slide under a microscope. Seth knew that they were trying to decide if that tingling at the back of their necks was because Bekah was a werewolf, or if it was from one of the other bodies.

"There is a lot of blood," Stripes admitted.

"Because she was eating deer!" Eleanor said impatiently. "She ran with the wolves. She's covered in blood. What other confirmation do we need? Let's get over this and shoot her."

Stripes gave an incredulous laugh. "Shoot her? Really? She's just a kid."

Jakob rolled his eyes. "You're such a sissy."

"Well, it's true! She's got to be, like, fourteen," he said. Yasir gave him a hard look. Stripes was too smart to challenge him. Instead, he stared at his feet as he shifted uncomfortably. "My sister's fourteen."

"Waste of Union funds," Eleanor muttered.

Yasir finally spoke up. He had been organizing their collection of teeth beside the camping stove and pretending to ignore them.

"We'll take her with us. We're almost to the mountain, and the moon is coming in a week. If she's a werewolf, she'll change sooner or later, and we can't leave a girl stranded in the meantime. If we get a late season snow, she'll die." Eleanor opened her mouth to argue, but Yasir stopped her. "That's my decision."

She got to her feet. "We should test how she responds to silver poisoning. Or cut her and see how she heals."

"No. We shot the others because we were already certain of their species. Not all werewolves heal quickly, either. It depends on how nourished they are."

SM Reine

"But—"

"Stripes is right. This one's a kid, probably younger than your son, and we don't have reason to think she's a werewolf. Remember that our primary mission is to protect humans. All of them."

"You're making a mistake," she said.

Yasir moved so fast that Seth actually jumped. He leaped to his feet and punched Eleanor across the face.

Her back hit the tree. A silver knife appeared in her hand instantly, and she lunged at him with a roar. Eleanor was terrifyingly fast, but even she was no match for the reflexes of a kopis with military training. He dodged out of the way before she hit.

She spun and lashed out a foot. It caught him in the gut. His breath gusted from him, but he caught her ankle.

With a swift motion, he pulled her off her feet. She landed with a grunt.

Yasir planted a boot in her chest and crouched. "Who's the commander?" he asked. Even though his voice was calm, his face was twisted into a look of hatred.

"I'm the specialist," Eleanor said without a hint of contrition. He leaned his weight on her chest, and bones creaked. She moved to stab him. He yanked the knife out of her hand.

"You didn't answer my question," Yasir said. "Who's the commander?"

"You are."

He let her stand. "We'll take the girl with us. You hear me? But if anyone sees her change—shoot her. Bed down, everyone. Tomorrow morning, we go to the mountain."

•○•

Seth waited until everyone was asleep before climbing into Jakob's SUV. He didn't close the door all the way so he could keep an eye on the sleeping bags outside.

Carefully, he unknotted Bekah's bindings. The motion made her stir. Bekah's eyes opened, and there was no recognition in her face. Only pure panic. Her wide eyes darted around the darkened car. She sounded like she was going to hyperventilate.

"What's going on? Who are you? Where am I?" Her words slurred over each other, as though she had forgotten how to talk like a human.

"Shh," Seth whispered, hoping she would take a hint from his volume. "Look at me, Bekah. It's me. It's Seth."

Confusion furrowed her brow. "Seth?"

"Yeah. It's all right. You're okay."

He helped her sit up against the seats. Once he was sure she wouldn't fall over, he let go. Bekah rubbed her eyes. Her hands left smudges of dirt on her face.

She gave him a trembling smile that was barely a ghost of her usual glow. "I can't believe it's you. I've been… lost… for a while. So I didn't expect to run into anyone I know. Did Rylie call you?"

Seth blinked. "You didn't come here with Rylie?"

"No. Didn't you?" Bekah frowned. "Where am I?"

"You're in the car of… uh, some friends of mine. We found you in the forest not far from Gray Mountain. Aren't you supposed to be at the sanctuary in California? How did you get all the way out here?"

"I've been having dreams about this mountain. On the last moon, when I changed… it was like I totally lost myself. I must have been wolfed out for hours. I woke up the next day miles from home without any of my friends, and I didn't know how to get back." Bekah shivered. "But I didn't *want* to go home. I hitched a ride with a family on an RV vacation. That's how I got across the country."

"Are you okay?"

"No. My leg hurts." She shuddered again, harder than before. "What's wrong with me, Seth?"

He held out his hands to calm her. "Let me look. Okay? I know a little first aid."

Bekah lifted her leg. Seth helped her clean off some of the blood and found a wound in the thickest part of her calf. One of those Union bullets had grazed her and left silver behind. The last time he had seen a similar wound, it had been on Rylie's thigh.

"It looks like there might be bullet fragments in your leg. I can remove them, but you have to be quiet. Can you keep from making any noise?" Seth asked. When she looked horrified by the suggestion, he nodded toward the sleeping bags outside. "We can't risk waking them up."

She went pale. "Okay. I guess." She made herself stare at the roof of the car and dug her fingers into the felt floor mat. "You have to help distract me. Tell me why I keep seeing this forest."

"Werewolves originally came from Gray Mountain," he said, grabbing a first aid kit out of the back, sterilizing his hands with alcohol, and opening sterile wipes. "Myth says that human settlers fought with the gods, and lycanthropy ended the war." He cleaned off the rest of the blood. "This is going to hurt a lot."

At her nod, he took a deep breath and dug his fingers into the wound on her calf. The bullet hadn't gone deep, so the first part was easy to find. Bekah bit her fist, but didn't cry out.

"All the werewolves are being called to the forest, so it's not just you," he went on, dropping the first fragment of bullet on a piece of gauze. "Nobody knows why or how, though."

She flapped her hands in the air as he extracted the second piece. Seth pocketed the bloody gauze so he could get rid of it. "Okay. You're done."

"Ouch," she whispered. "But… it's burning. That's good." As they watched, the edges of the injury began to close.

"We'll have to bandage this," he said, cleaning up the blood he had smeared on her. After a short moment, she was totally healed, and the only sign something had happened was a red mark like a fading bruise. The wound wasn't as bad as Rylie's had been after all. "The Union can't know you were shot, and they definitely can't know that you've healed from it. So if anyone asks, you tripped in the forest and scraped yourself. Got it?"

"I've got it. Who are you traveling with?" she asked below her breath, eyeballing the sleeping bags through the window. "What's 'the Union'?"

Seth gave her a short summary. Bekah didn't need much detail—she was smart enough to infer that the situation was bad.

"So you're saying this is an extermination force," she said.

"Pretty much." He grimaced at the faint silhouette of the mountain against the sky. "There are supposed to be more of them on the mountain. And I'm expecting for us to run into more werewolves as we get close to the next moon, too."

"This is bad. This is really bad," Bekah said.

"You don't have to tell me that."

"What are we going to do?"

Seth ran through a list of options in his mind: Panic. Run away. Kill the Union in their sleep. Panic *and* run away. Find Rylie and Abel and probably dozens of other wolves. Or confront whatever was calling them to the mountain and get caught in a slaughter.

None of that was especially inspirational, and judging by Bekah's terrified eyes, she really needed inspiration.

"Well, first, I'm going to sleep. I'm wasted." He made himself smile even though he didn't feel it. He wrapped the bandages around her leg and pinned them in place. "I could let you out of here. It would be safer than staying with us. If they find out what you are..." Seth trailed off and tried not to look toward the rifles mounted behind the driver's seat. He failed. To her credit, Bekah only looked a little bit terrified.

"But they would know that you did it." She shook her head. "No. I can fake it for now. I'll come up with a story and slip away when they're watching you, so they know you didn't set me free. And I know Levi will come for me. He won't let them hurt me."

He patted her hand. "Yeah, I'm sure he's not far away."

Seth wasn't sure if that was a comforting thought or not. Bekah's weak smile seemed to indicate agreement.

"You'd better tie me back up," she said, and she lay down.

He knotted the ropes around her wrists and ankles the way they had been before. "We passed a car on the way here. You should tell them that's how you got to the forest. Okay?" She nodded. Seth climbed out of the SUV again. "Try to get some sleep."

She rested her head on her arms. "Thanks. And Seth?" He paused halfway out the door. "Rylie's going to be fine. I'm sure of it."

His stomach knotted just thinking about it. "Yeah," he said with more confidence than he felt. "Me too."

He silently slid the door of the SUV closed.

When he turned around, Eleanor was watching him.

Her sleeping bag was open and unzipped, and he had been too busy with Bekah to notice that she had gotten up. Eleanor probably hadn't gone to sleep in the first place. There was no way she could have heard their conversation through the SUV's door. They had been whispering, and she didn't have a werewolf's hearing. But she looked suspicious.

He immediately felt guilty. Her glare had a way of making him feel like that. "Mom," he said, just to break the silence of the night.

She sat on the hood of the opposite SUV, running a sharpening stone along the business end of her silver-tipped knife. "How's the girl doing?"

"She's awake. I heard her moving around and wanted to see what she could tell me."

"And?"

"And she was driving through and got in a wreck. That was her car." He wondered if his mother could hear his pulse racing. It took all of his control to keep his voice totally calm. "She's not a werewolf. I helped bandage her up myself."

"Hmm," Eleanor said. She held up the blade and tilted it to catch the starlight. She spit on it, rubbed it on her jeans, and looked again.

"What are you doing awake?"

"I'm looking out for werewolves... and werewolf sympathizers." Even in the darkness, her black eyes were sharp.

"I'm going to sleep, Mom," he said, even though he could imagine all too clearly that blade plunging into his sleeping bag to bury into his back.

"You look scared," Eleanor said.

"I'm tired."

She waved the knife in the air. "Don't worry. This isn't for you, boy. This is for the wolves." She jabbed the blade at the other SUV. "Tell me, Seth. Haven't I been a good mother?"

"Are you looking for an honest answer? Or are you just feeling pensive tonight?"

"Tell me the truth," she said. "I kept a roof over your head. I kept you fed and dressed. I trained you to fight and survive in a hard world that wants you dead. I gave you boys everything I had of myself—my life, my body, my soul—and for what? An ungrateful punk who would rather drive cross-country with a stranger in his car instead of his mother."

"You tied me up and threw me under our mobile home," Seth said dully.

"I protected you."

"You dragged my girlfriend behind a motorcycle."

That got a reaction. She dropped to her feet and advanced on Seth. "She's a monster," Eleanor hissed.

He glanced over at the sleeping bags. Nobody stirred, but he was pretty sure they had an audience. There was no way anyone could sleep through that. Seth lowered his tone. "Rylie's not the one who dropped poisoned meat in a school."

"All for your protection." She bit out the last word.

"Did you ever think I didn't want to be protected?" He gathered all his resolve and stood toe-to-toe with Eleanor. "No. That's the answer to your question. You *haven't* been a good mother. You've been mean. You've been a bully. You might have kept us dressed, but it was in uniform so we would march in your stupid army. You taught us to kill innocent people. You housed us in motels while you chased Dad's dreams."

"You deserved worse," Eleanor whispered. "I should have left you under the trailer."

"It takes a lot more than fur and fangs to make a monster. That's all I'm saying, Mom."

"And I know why you're here. I know what you plan to do. I'm watching you."

Seth sighed. "Okay. What am I planning to do?"

"You're going to kill them all in their sleep. The Union. And you're going to run off with the wolves."

He had to laugh. "I'm not a killer, Mom. Not anymore. Not since I escaped from you." He took another look at the sleeping bags. One of them had shifted. Was that Yasir? He raised his voice a little. "But we can end everything here. If all the werewolves die, there won't be any more attacks. No more victims. And I want this to end as much as you do."

"I wish I believed you. I really wish I did. But I hear your lies, and so does God, and you're going to be judged. You ought to know that."

He rubbed a hand over his face. "Goodnight, Mom."

"I'll be watching," she whispered.

Eleven

The Shores of Golden Lake

Rylie opened her eyes on blue sky and a single drifting cloud.

She smelled pine trees. Fresh water. Stone encrusted with winter's ice. The crisp bite of spring air. There was something wet beneath her flexing fingertips that felt like sand, and her legs were damp.

She sat up. Sand squished underneath her.

Rylie lay on the shores of Golden Lake. The early morning light cast a yellow haze over the sky, though the trees were still heavy with the violet shadows of nighttime, and trees that had been growing for centuries towered overhead. There was a rock face behind her. If she climbed it, she knew she would see a path, and if she followed that path, there would be cabins.

She twisted, and her gaze tracked up the slope to the mountain and its bald peaks still marked with white snow.

Gray Mountain.

"I'm dreaming," she whispered, "I have to be dreaming…"

She got to her feet and spun around, searching for the body in the waves. Water slopped over her feet. Her legs must have been in the lake for a long time, because she couldn't even feel it on her toes. But the surf was empty of everything except colorful rocks worn smooth by years of waves. The trees rustled with a breeze that blew the hair back from her face.

Rylie ran her hands down her body. She was naked, but uninjured.

Why was she naked? What happened?

"I have to be dreaming," she repeated, more firmly this time. A fresh breeze blew, and she shivered as chilly waves rippled over her skin. That didn't feel like a dream breeze.

She lifted her nose to the breeze and took a short sniff. Those weren't dream smells, nor were they the faint echoes of Gray Mountain that she always picked up off other werewolves. It was the real thing. The wolf inside her recognized it, and it filled her with a powerful sense of calm and peace.

Rylie wasn't far from Camp Silver Brook.

She climbed the rock face, digging in her fingers and toes for traction. It had been a long time since campers scrambled over the beach while enjoying warm summer days, so the moss had grown thick and slimy. It was tough getting a grip. But she was much stronger than she had been the year before, so it didn't take much effort to get over the cliff.

A winding dirt path led into the trees, just as she expected. She could make out the hard lines of what had once been the office building through the bushes. There was a sign by the path. One arrow pointed to a path parallel to the lake's shore and said, "Archery Range." Beneath that was another arrow that said, "Stables." And the third arrow was aimed at the buildings. It said, "Camp Silver Brook."

Her throat clenched shut, and her hands flew to her mouth as her eyes began to burn.

She hadn't thought about where she was driving with Abel over the last couple of days. Not really. But now that she was there, she couldn't deny it anymore.

It wasn't a dream. She was really at Camp Silver Brook.

She sank to her knees and began to cry.

The stress of the long months away from Seth and Aunt Gwyn finally caught up with her. The stress of killing people, and the pain of shapeshifting into a wolf's body. Her dad's passing. The regret of watching those people die at camp. Losing everything she cared about in her life. And once she let the tears flow, they didn't stop. She sobbed into her hands and watched the dirt absorb her tears.

The grief wasn't enough to summon the wolf. It liked to feed off her anger and fear, not her sadness. But her skin prickled impatiently. Now that she was on Gray Mountain, the wolf wanted to move, to hunt, to climb to the peak and find what had been calling to it for weeks.

She felt like gravity had tripled. She couldn't move.

Footsteps shuffled on the path. Rylie looked up, and through bleary eyes, she saw a familiar figure wearing a black t-shirt and jeans. For an instant, she thought it was Seth. That was the first place she had seen him—she had been sitting outside the office, and he had paddled past in a canoe stolen from the recreation shed on the boys' side of the lake. But when she wiped the tears out of her eyes, she recognized Abel's broad shoulders and scarred cheek.

He sat down next to her, but politely kept his eyes toward the lake. He wasn't nice about many things, but he had always been nice about respecting Rylie's modesty. It might have helped that Scott enforced a pretty strict "don't be creepy about sky-clad werewolves" rule at the sanctuary. She liked to think it was because she was growing on him.

"Glad to see you're okay," he said.

She sniffled hard. "I'm cold."

It made her feel a little better when he rolled his eyes. "Can't you try hanging on to your clothes for longer than a few hours? Jeez." But he removed his t-shirt and handed it over. The unscarred side of his bare chest pebbled with cold.

Rylie tugged it over her head. Abel was so big that the shirt was more like a dress, and it almost brushed her dirty knees. "Thanks," she said. She was still crying hard enough that it took her two tries to speak.

"Whatever."

There was a little more bitterness in his tone than usual, and his face was carved with hard, angry lines. He would probably pick on her if she asked what he was thinking about, so she asked, "Where's the car?"

"We left it in the forest five miles back. *Someone* broke the windshield."

"Five miles? Wow." She looked down at her bare legs and couldn't even work up the energy to blush. "Can we look for clothes? The shirt is kinda breezy, and I'm not hiking back to the car without shoes. Or pants. Or underwear."

"Wimp," Abel said.

Rylie was ready for his insult. "Troll," she shot back.

"Troll? That's the best you could come up with? You suck."

"Shut up and help me break into the office."

Normally, that should have earned a laugh from him, but he just grunted.

She distracted herself from the growing presence of the wolf, and the accompanying anxiety clenching low in her belly, by looking for the biggest rock she could find. Rylie picked up a rock the size of her fist, but dropped it when she saw another the size of a softball.

They stood side by side in front of the empty office. One of the windows had already been shattered and was covered in boards. The door was padlocked.

"What makes you think there are clothes in the office?" Abel asked.

She swallowed hard. "That's where they kept the lost and found."

Hefting the rock in her hand, she hurled it at the remaining window. It shattered. The experience was way too satisfying.

Abel punched his arm through the glass, clearing out a hole big enough for them to fit through. He got a little scraped up in the process, but by the time they were both inside, he had healed again.

The last time Rylie had been in the office, she had been in trouble for stealing a counselor's car to sneak into the boys' camp. The walls were still covered in the same kitschy posters. The mini-fridge stood open and empty. Papers were scattered across the desk. Everyone had left in a big hurry.

A closet in the back served as the lost and found. Rylie searched through boxes for clothes that would fit and came up with an ugly pair of shorts, hiking boots that were a size too big, and a yellow tank top that bagged around the chest and arms.

She shut the door and changed in total darkness. When she emerged to give Abel his shirt back, he didn't even laugh at her horrible outfit.

"Okay, I give up. What's wrong?" Rylie asked. "Did I eat someone last night?"

He snorted. "I wish you had."

"That's not funny."

"I wasn't trying to be funny." He put his shirt back on, and Rylie stared at him, waiting for an answer to her question. He sighed and flopped into the chair behind the front desk. "Two werewolves got shot last night. I found the third one dead in the woods a mile east of here while you were still chasing bunny rabbits. Kind of looked like a blood vessel in her brain popped or something."

"Who would shoot someone out here?" she asked. "We're miles from the city. The nearest people are at the ranger station, and they wouldn't shoot a wolf... would they? Not with silver bullets, for sure."

"They weren't rangers." His voice heated. "They were hunters."

A chill ran through her. "Oh."

"Yeah, 'oh.' Thanks for adding to the conversation."

Rylie crossed her arms over her chest. "Well, sorry I humored you and went on your stupid spontaneous road trip to Gray Mountain! It's not like I'm *adding anything* to the experience. I should have just stayed home."

Abel stayed seated. His whole face was twisted with anger, but it was not directed at her. He didn't even seem to hear her outburst. "They had these big black SUVs with antenna and floodlights and stuff. Expensive equipment. They chased the werewolves down. And… I saw one of them give chase on foot." He glanced at her. "That hunter went after you specifically."

"Well, he obviously wasn't very good. I'm fine." She spread her arms wide. "We can deal with hunters."

"It's not that," Abel said.

"Then what?"

He paused for a long time, like he was trying to decide if he really wanted to say what he was thinking or not. Abel heaved a deep breath and gave Rylie a very serious look. She had never seen him look quite that somber before.

"The hunter was Seth."

Twelve

Outpost

"Where is she?"

Yasir's roar woke Seth up with a jolt. He sat upright in his sleeping bag and stared around the forest with bleary eyes.

Morning had dawned fresh and bright over the mountain. Stripes was still sleeping on the other side of the miniature camping stove, which was currently heating a pot of unidentifiable Union rations, but Jakob and Yasir were both awake. They were tearing through camp. Yasir flung open the doors to the SUV and kicked over a stack of crates they had temporarily unloaded to provide shelter.

Seth got to his feet and dusted off. "What's wrong?" he asked, keeping his voice neutral.

Yasir rounded on him. His fist was clenched so tightly on a shotgun that his knuckles were pale. "She's gone! That woman is gone!"

And then Seth noticed a pair of round, frightened eyes from the open door of the SUV behind the commander. Bekah's curls were always wild, but bed-head made her look extra crazy that morning. But she was still there. Seth had been half-certain that she would have left.

So if Bekah hadn't run away in the middle of the night...

His fear turned to dread.

"Eleanor," Seth said.

Yasir wheeled around to shout into the forest. "Eleanor!" His call bounced off the slopes and came back at them threefold. A flock of birds exploded from the trees.

Gone.

What could it mean? Why would she leave without telling them?

Seth did a quick search of the camp, but he couldn't find his father's book, his mother's gun, or anything else she had brought along. One of the backpacks was missing, too. She must have gotten up in the early hours and left while everyone was sleeping.

Yasir whirled on Bekah. She paled under his glare. "Did you see anything?"

"I saw someone leave this morning, but it was pretty dark. I couldn't tell who it was," she said in a tiny voice.

"Was it a woman? What did she take?"

"I don't know. I'm sorry." She glanced nervously between the men. "Can I go now?"

Yasir ignored her plea.

Stripes zipped up his pants as he walked out of the forest and wiped his hands clean on his shirt. "Good riddance," he said, yawning. The anger and disgust in Yasir's eyes said that he didn't agree.

"Was she not supposed to leave?" Seth asked. "It's not like she was a prisoner, right?"

The commander's brows knitted together. The expression spoke a thousand words. "Come here, kid," he said, snapping his fingers. "Help me search outside the camp. Stripes, Jakob— pack up! We're getting out of here in ten minutes. You hear me?"

Seth followed Yasir far enough away that the other men wouldn't be able to hear. But they didn't search. Both of them had already come to the same conclusion: Eleanor was long gone.

With his arms folded, Yasir's biceps were each as big around as a tree, and corded with veins. "Your mother raided a Union camp. She stole a lot of things. Vandalized a library. They were going to press charges against her—not with the police; we go by our own laws—but when they realized that she was married to the guy who wrote the book on werewolves, they decided to put her to good use instead. They told her it was cooperation or a prison camp. So…" He gave a stiff shrug.

"So she wasn't a team member. You were keeping an eye on her."

"Something like that." He threw his hands in the air. "She hadn't shown any signs of running for weeks! She agreed to go peacefully as long as we let her reunite with her son and kill werewolves, and we've done both. I was sure that she would be easy to control once we had you." His fist cracked into his palm. "I should have never let my guard down!"

"You can't blame yourself. My mom's clever," Seth said.

"She's a conniving snake. That's what she is."

He didn't argue. That was as good a description of Eleanor as anything else. "My guess? She wanted you to get her to the mountain. Otherwise, she would have escaped weeks ago."

"Oh yeah? If you understand her so well, then tell me, kid: Where did she go? What's she doing?"

He turned to stare at the distant peak of Gray Mountain touched by morning sunlight. The birds were silent in the trees, making it eerily still. He tried to think like his mother thought. He had seen her go through what she called "the process" so many times that he could have emulated her methods in his sleep.

"You said she wanted to reunite with her son and kill werewolves," Seth said slowly. Yasir nodded impatiently.

Eleanor tried to put herself in the position of werewolves when she hunted. She knew how they lived and where to find them. She could predict their behaviors as easily as Seth could predict hers.

But if she wanted to kill werewolves, the best way to do it would have been to stay with the Union. So if she ran away, it would be to do something that they didn't want her to do—or something she knew Seth wouldn't let her do.

A terrible thought entered his mind. It was so bad he didn't even want to contemplate it. "Eleanor has two sons. She probably didn't mention that, because my brother is a werewolf," Seth said. "He's likely to come here, too."

"You think she's going to try to save him?" Yasir asked, eyes narrowing with calculation. He was probably trying to decide if that could be Seth's motivation, too.

"No. I'm pretty sure she wants to kill him."

• ○ •

It soon turned out that Eleanor hadn't just vanished in the night. She had also employed what Abel had taught her about mechanics to disable the SUVs.

Yasir stared under the hood of the car at the severed tubes. "I'm going to shoot her."

"You'll have to catch her first. What do we do?" Seth asked.

"We walk." He slammed the hood shut. "Another unit has established an outpost halfway up the mountain. It's ten miles uphill—not a very long drive. Too bad about the cars." He delivered a vicious kick to the tire.

While everybody else loaded backpacks, Jakob backtracked to look for the place they had abandoned the Chevelle. He returned an hour later while they were still trying to cram one more laptop into an overstuffed backpack. "I found Chevelle's tracks, but the vehicle is gone," he reported. "Eleanor must have taken it."

Yasir swore fluently in a language Seth didn't recognize or understand. He could tell it was pretty foul without understanding it.

Everybody loaded themselves down with a backpack of the necessities—even Bekah—and left the rest behind.

It was a very long hike up the mountain.

Whatever training the Union put their hunters through must have been pretty good. Seth thought he was in great shape. Bekah wasn't exactly a couch potato, either. But they could barely keep up with the rest of the unit. The men powered through the forest at top speed despite carrying fifty-pound backpacks.

When Seth and Bekah fell behind for the third time, he whispered, "You could run now."

She was red-faced and breathing hard. "They'll blame you."

"Who knows what the Union outpost will be like? You should go."

"Don't worry about me. I'm fine." She gave him that big smile.

"Hurry up, kids!" Yasir shouted back at them. And then they were walking too fast to keep talking at all.

They were on the same side of the lake as the boys' camp, but they took a straight path up the mountain and avoided the cabins. The quality of the air changed as they increased in elevation. It grew thinner and colder. The ground got muddier, and then he saw actual patches of snow. His feet stuck to the ground with every step.

The trees began thinning again. He spotted a glimmer of water over the side of the trail.

Breaking away from the rest of the group, he walked up to the edge and took a long look at Golden Lake as the midday sun rose overhead. He remembered standing on that exact point the previous summer. The cabins would be pinpricks of yellow at night, like stars that had fallen into the trees.

He wondered if Rylie was down there yet.

Someone yelled at him. He hiked the backpack higher on his shoulders and rushed to catch up.

They reached the outpost an hour later.

The Union had established their base in the ruins of an old settlement. When Seth had been there last time, a fence had kept people out of the historical site, but the Union had torn it down and replaced it with a perimeter of floodlights. They took over the ruins of the stone church, parked a half-dozen SUVs under the trees, and positioned two large RVs in back. Seth couldn't imagine how they had gotten those up the mountain without a helicopter.

The Union had also dug a trench to protect their supplies. There was even a full-fledged forge where they melted silver. It was more than just an outpost. They had built a small town for themselves.

Seth stared at everything with his mouth agape. There must have been a dozen kopides working at the outpost. He hadn't even realized that there were that many hunters in the whole world.

Yasir laughed when he saw Seth's expression. "Impressed?"

"This is… wow. How much money does the Union have?"

"Enough," he said.

Seth really was impressed. But he was also scared. How were the werewolves supposed to stand a chance against those kinds of forces? An ugly memory of Rylie tied up in the church came to mind, and he knew that the Union wouldn't let her get that far again if they caught her. The men walking the perimeter had big guns and hard faces. The kind of people who shot on sight.

If Seth was kind of scared, then Bekah was downright terrified. He realized she wasn't next to him anymore and turned around to see her standing back by the trees.

He went back to get her. "Come on. Keep walking."

"There's so much silver," she whispered. Her eyes were watering. "I don't feel very good."

Seth glanced around. Nobody was close enough to hear them, but Yasir would look for them as soon as he realized they had fallen behind again. He took her backpack. "Deep breaths. You can't change."

She laughed shakily. "I'm not Rylie. And don't you think deep breaths would be a bad idea with all the silver in the air?"

A little embarrassed, he grinned. "It sounded like a good idea."

"Thanks. Really. But I'm fine."

Bekah squared her shoulders and followed him into the Union outpost.

Yasir's unit was waiting by the stone church while the commander spoke with another man. It was hard to tell if he was also a commander because everyone in the Union wore black. "Who's that?" asked the new man, nodding toward Seth and Bekah.

"The guy is Eleanor's kid," Yasir said. He spoke her name like a swear word. "The girl's a potential thirty-twenty. We found her south of here, but there's no confirmation. Do we have a holding pen yet?"

She looked at Seth. "Thirty-twenty?" she echoed quietly. He shrugged.

"We're locking them in the church," said the Union member. "Pretty pathetic lot. We've only picked up three so far. Toss her in and drop off your stuff. We're laying silver traps today."

"Got it." Yasir snapped his fingers at Bekah. "You. In the church. Now."

"I just want to go home," she said.

"Sorry. You're camping for the next week. Move it."

She gave Seth a last helpless look. He leaned in close to whisper, "If you get a chance, don't wait around. Run."

Bekah didn't acknowledge that he had spoken. She mounted the steps to the church, wavering a little on her feet, and took a deep breath. She went inside and was sealed away from the rest of the world.

Yasir clapped his hands. "All right, everyone. Drop your bags in the tent. It's time to start the real work."

Thirteen

Advent of Wolves

Rylic and Abel found a series of caves on the beach north of the campgrounds. They picked one in the middle to be home base. It wasn't much of a cave at all—more like a place where the rocks had slipped to make a sheltered area. They had to walk through calf-deep water to reach it, but it was dry and flat inside, and protected from the wind.

"I'm going to find the car and recover the duffel bag," Abel said. "You need to locate supplies." When she looked at him blankly, he rolled his eyes. "You know. Blankets, pillows, towels, canned food. *Supplies*. It's not that hard. Go figure it out."

"What if we run into Seth?"

Abel's face was hard. "Then we'll deal with him."

They hadn't talked much about Seth. Even though her wolf should have been exhausted after the previous night's run, finding out that he was with hunters had been upsetting enough to make her start changing. She managed to get control of herself before she went four-legged, but discussing the issue of Seth didn't seem worth the risk.

But they were both thinking about him. She could tell by the slant to Abel's mouth and the tension in his shoulders. He never said it, but he loved his brother, and running into him on the hunt must have hurt.

She wanted to believe it was some kind of a mistake—that maybe, somehow, Abel was just imagining things. But if Abel *had* seen his brother, and if Seth really was with the hunters that had killed three werewolves, there must have been a good reason. Rylie didn't believe he would turn against them. Not Seth.

Her wolf stirred at the thought again, so she put Seth out of her mind. She had gotten good at that lately.

"Watch out for yourself," Abel said, crouched at the mouth of their little cave.

He left, and a few minutes later, she left too.

Rylie found a laundry bag in the front office and put anything that looked useful into it. She skipped pens and paper and other office supplies. Instead, she broke into a box of towels branded with the camp logo and took a handful. Then she located the laundry facilities by following the scent of bleach and started gathering pillows and blankets.

Once her bag was half-filled by linens, she went to the back entrance for the kitchens. Nothing in the walk-in refrigerator was good. It had been unplugged, and everything was worse than rancid. It was practically sentient. She didn't even have to open the door to know that. It reeked through the gaps. But the canned food looked good, and it wasn't hard to dig up a can opener.

Rylie tossed it all into her bag, keeping an eye on the dining room through the double doors. The windows were so dirty that it made the big room feel like a gloomy cavern.

And then something dark moved in the mess hall.

She wasn't alone.

Adrenaline shot through her veins. *An enemy in my territory. Fight. Kill.*

She held her breath. Closed her eyes. Counted slowly to ten. It wasn't easy forcing her human thoughts to dominate those of the wolf, so she spoke aloud to herself. "It's probably a raccoon looking for food," she whispered. Or a bear—but if that was the case, then she would have to keep shapeshifting as an option after all.

Dropping her bag by the door, Rylie crept out into the mess hall. Everything was where she remembered leaving it. The tables were still lined up in the center of the room. The buffet line was dusty, and the food that had been left in the trays had long since dried out. Whatever it was, the damage of time was so bad that even her sensitive nose couldn't tell what it used to be.

But her nose did pick up another smell. A living one.

Rylie stood in the center of the room, watching for another hint of movement. The wolf wanted to hunt, but she pushed it back. She would react like a human would and be civil.

"Hello?" she called, her voice quavering as the wolf seized her throat. She took a deep breath before saying, "Who's there?"

Something bumped against a table at the back of the room. Slowly, a human figure stood.

It was a woman. She looked like she was probably in her mid-twenties, but shorter than Rylie. Her skin was the color of coconut milk and her black hair fell in straight lines to her shoulders. She also looked very, very confused, and judging by the way she wasn't wearing any clothes, it was probably because she had been wandering through the forest since the last moon.

She said something. It sounded like Japanese or Chinese. Rylie didn't understand a word of it.

"It's okay," Rylie said, holding out her hands with fingers spread. Her nails were itching, but she made herself ignore it. "I'm not going to hurt you." *Not on purpose, anyway.*

The woman spoke again, arms folded over her chest. She hung her head.

"Here. Let me get you a shirt."

Rylie moved for the laundry bag. The woman dropped into a half-squat, teeth bared in a growl.

Her wolf reacted by sweeping to the surface, and it momentarily consumed her thoughts. The sweeping musk of pheromones washed over her. They may not have shared a human language, but the smells were more than enough.

The woman had been through the creek. She had walked through mud and pine and slept in dens made of soil. But before that, she had been on an airplane. Rylie recognized a faint whiff of stale, recycled air. The other smells were too old to distinguish, but everything about the woman smelled of places Rylie had never been, and it was interesting enough to the wolf to quell some of the aggression. Especially when the woman finally dropped her hands and closed her mouth.

"I'm going to get you a shirt," she said again, speaking slower and louder than before, like that would actually cross the language barrier. Rylie tugged on her own shirt.

"Toshiko *desu*," said the woman.

"Shirt?"

"*Watashi no namae wa* Toshiko *desu*."

Rylie frowned. "Okay… hang on. Just a second."

She fished an extra shirt and shorts out of her laundry bag. She had made her selections based on her own size, but the other woman was much smaller. Rylie set the clothes on a table between them and backed away.

The woman dressed. "*Arigatou*."

"My name is Rylie." She patted her chest. "Rylie. *Rylie*. What's your name?"

Mimicking the chest pat, she said, "Toshiko. Toshiko *desu*."

What she was trying to say finally registered. "Oh. Your name is Toshiko, isn't it?" Rylie pointed at herself, and then to the woman as she dressed. "Rylie. Toshiko. Right?"

Toshiko nodded encouragingly, although Rylie couldn't tell if that was because she was happy to have the clothes, or if she actually understood what was happening. After she was fully dressed, she pointed to the door and said something else. She seemed to want Rylie to follow her.

Shouldering her laundry bag, Rylie followed the other werewolf at a distance. Outside, she could see that Toshiko was filthy. Her feet were covered in dried blood, and so were her hands. Judging by the smells, only some of it was her blood. Rylie had to stop and take a few deep breaths to quell her inner wolf again. It didn't like that someone else had been eating. It wanted to be the first to eat, always, and to have its teeth in every kill.

"Get over yourself," Rylie muttered.

Toshiko looked askance at her, but she only shook her head.

They walked for a few minutes over familiar trails to other cabins. Toshiko led her to the place where Group C had slept, and pointed at each of the cabins while speaking. She talked slowly and loudly, too. It didn't make any difference. But Rylie didn't need to speak a foreign language to get what she was saying.

"There are others here?"

The woman nodded with wide eyes, not quite as enthusiastic as she had been before.

A door opened. Rylie's hackles rose as a man stepped outside. He was as naked and dirty as Toshiko had been.

"Back off!" he growled with a thick brogue, eyes flashing.

She dropped her bag. She couldn't hold on to it anymore. The wolf had no idea what to do with hands. "Be careful. Please don't provoke me," she responded. Her voice was deep again, and her spine creaked. Her lower back ached as an extra vertebra or two tried to grind into place.

"My territory. Mine!"

Rylie quickly sized up the situation. He was a pretty big guy—not as wide as Abel, but almost as tall. His red hair was a mess. He had a good amount of muscle. She didn't think she could take him... as a human.

Her whole body shuddered. She doubled over with a groan.

He seemed to take it as a sign of weakness. He crossed the distance between them and swung a fist.

Distracted by the pain of a changing body, she couldn't dodge it. The blow connected with her face. She sprawled back on the dirt with a cry that was only half-surprise—her kneecaps snapped simultaneously, and she was so shocked she couldn't find the mental control to stop it.

Toshiko ran between them, waving her arms, but that only got her a right hook across the face, too. She went flying.

Rylie barely saw it. Pain consumed her.

Her skin was on fire, her fingernails were bleeding, and blood sprayed as her face extended into a wolf's jaw. The change had accelerated as she had matured in the last few months, so everything happened at once with a blur of pain.

All her hair was gone in a heartbeat. Her ears crunched and slid to the top of her head. Her new clothing ripped at the seams. She flipped onto her belly and dug her fingers into the dirt as they shortened into paws. A tail lashed from the base of her spine. Rylie found her footing on hind legs that had reversed direction, and wailed as the fur erupted across her fleshy pink skin.

Only a minute later, a wolf stood in the middle of the cabins.

It looked at the man, who had frozen next to the charcoal that used to be a campfire, and it liked its chances against him.

"No," he said. "That's not possible."

She jumped on him.

Her momentum carried both of them to the ground, and the wolf clamped its jaws on his arm when he flung it in front of his face. She worried it in her teeth like a chew toy. The taste of blood washed over her tongue as he screamed.

"Let me go!"

He punched her again. Even as a human, he was pretty strong, and that distinctly human move surprised her. She moved enough for him to scramble to his feet and break into a run. The wolf loped after him.

The man dodged her attempt at a tackle. The bleeding of the wound on his arm was already slowing.

Toshiko yelled next to them. Her voice cut through the wolf's focus.

Don't hurt her.

A ripple ran through the wolf's body, and it hesitated. That inner voice was growing stronger. In the middle of the day, so soon after the last change, the wolf was already weak. And Rylie desperately didn't want to hurt anyone. The urge was so powerful that it completely shattered the wolf's focus.

She sat on her haunches and tried to shake the voice out of her head. It didn't help.

Let me go. Let me turn back.

The man watched her warily, fists at the ready.

It hurt more than usual to shift back to her human shape. Usually, the wolf hung onto her consciousness until it was over. But it slipped away quickly and quietly, leaving Rylie to face it on her own.

"Jesus, Mary, and Joseph," said the man when she finished changing.

He moved for her. Rylie held up a hand to stop him. "Don't come near me! I could have killed you."

"I wasn't going to attack again." He laughed with disbelief. He was a lot calmer now that he had a couple big chunks bitten out of his arm, though they had grown back completely. "I'm not stupid. Do you want a hand up?"

"I bit you."

He shrugged. "I attacked first. Are we good?"

"I guess so," Rylie said.

"Need help up?"

She took his hand. She picked up the tangled scraps of her clothes, but they were too destroyed to put back on. Good thing she had taken a lot of clothes out of the lost and found.

The others waited in awkward silence as she dressed.

"Sorry about the arm," she said when she finished. "I don't meet new werewolves very often, and I kind of have… control problems."

"I think we all do," he said. Toshiko didn't seem to be listening. She picked through Rylie's laundry bag, found a bag of trail mix, and tore it open. She dug into it like it was a turkey dinner instead of stale almonds and cranberries.

"When is the last time you guys ate?" Rylie asked.

He had to think too hard about it. "When was the last change? We've been eating a couple of deer we killed."

So that explained all the blood. "Have you seen others?"

"Yeah. I've come across three other groups, but they're all out there somewhere now." He nodded toward the trees. "Been picking a lot of fights, to tell you the truth. Can't seem to help it—I lose my brain for a few minutes when I smell someone new. That's the first time I didn't win." He rubbed his arm. "You're not like me."

Rylie laughed shakily. "Yeah. And no. I can explain, but not here. There are hunters on the mountain, and they're probably going to search the camps."

He frowned. "For what?"

"For us."

"What?" His eyes widened and his mouth dropped open. He spun around to stare at the forest, like he expected an army of hunters to march through right that second. "But… why?"

"Because they're werewolf hunters, and we're werewolves, and they want us all dead. They think we're monsters."

"I'm not a monster. I'm just Irish."

Rylie didn't really know what to say to that. She was "just" some high school girl who had been bitten at summer camp, too, but she was also a monster. The first thing didn't seem to matter much when the second thing came into play.

Changing the subject seemed a lot easier than trying to explain the hunters. "I have clothes that should probably fit you in the bag, too. Hang on." Rylie dug out the baggiest shorts. He looked skeptical, but put them on. They didn't even reach halfway down his hairy thighs. "My friend will bring more clothes with him. You can borrow something better."

"A friend, eh? Where's this 'friend'?"

"He's looking for our car. But we're camping in caves by the lake. I think you and Toshiko should come with me."

"Toshiko?"

The Asian woman looked up from shaking the bag of trail mix into her mouth. Rylie's brow furrowed. "Isn't that her name?"

"I don't understand a bleeding thing she says. She started following me around when I got here and I can't shake her," he said. When Rylie opened her mouth to ask Toshiko to leave with them, he shook his head. "Don't bother. She talks nonsense."

"I think it's Chinese, actually," she said.

But it turned out he was right. They didn't have to talk to Toshiko to get her to follow. Rylie picked up her bag and started walking for the beach, and the other werewolf followed.

"So what's the plan?" he asked as they shuffled along.

Rylie's eyebrows lifted. "Why are you asking me?"

"I dunno. You've got the cave and the clothes and the news about the hunters. I expected you to have a plan, too."

She grimaced at the peak of Gray Mountain. The sun was creeping toward it. She hadn't given it any thought to what she would do once she got there. She had kind of hoped she would run into someone else with a plan. Or even better—someone with answers. But it was becoming more and more obvious that everyone was as clueless as she was.

"Sorry," she said. "I can't help with that."

Fourteen

The Ruined Church

Seth thought it would be hard to get away from the Union once he was entrenched in their compound, but with Eleanor gone, they pretty much ignored him. Nobody even looked at him twice when he went wandering around the ruined settlement the next day.

The Union must have had a ton of money. Yasir said they had only been there since the new moon, but they had built themselves a small city. They had a tented mess hall, exercise equipment, and all kinds of monitoring devices.

The trackers in the SUVs were only the beginning of their technology. He peered through the open door of an RV to study their huge monitors, and saw they had an enlarged map of the forest with an overlay of patchwork colors. A woman in uniform sat in front of the monitors. Judging by her silver jewelry, she must have been one of the witches assigned to the team.

"What's everything in the RV for?" Seth asked Stripes, who was seated on the grass nearby to eat a can of beans for dinner.

"Motion detectors." He waved his fork in the air. "They've been putting them in the trees. See that number? That's an estimate of the number of animals in the forest. The lower number is how many of those the computer thinks are werewolves." The number of animals was in the thousands; the second number was fifty-six.

"It looks for unusual human movement patterns. We've tagged a couple of werewolves, too, so we can follow the groups that way. Union uniforms have trackers, so we don't count."

A knot of worry grew in Seth's stomach as he watched the blinking lights travel across the screens. "How many werewolves are here, in the compound?"

"There are four in the church we haven't confirmed yet. I think we killed twelve others, but you'd have to check the teeth hanging in the supply tent to be sure."

The idea was nauseating. "So you guys are picking off wolves while they're human after all?"

"Only if we've seen them shift, or if we have a recording of them healing a major wound. We'll do a sweep tomorrow to pick up a few more, but we'll wait until the next moon to finish them off." Stripes looked bored by the conversation. He scraped his fork at the bottom of the can, knocked the remaining beans into his mouth, and belched. "I'm going back for seconds."

The witch glanced back at Seth in the doorway when Stripes left. "Move on," she snapped.

Seth jumped down, but he didn't know where to go. It would be too easy to track him. He squinted at the branches in the falling light of evening. He didn't *see* any sensors, but he wasn't sure if it was because they didn't monitor camp, or because they were too well hidden.

Could he use the monitors to find Eleanor? Or even better—could he find Rylie?

He wandered across the field, watching the men forge silver from a distance. The stone church's crumbling walls caught his gaze. If there were four werewolves in the church, and one of them was Bekah, then who were the other three?

Seth intercepted a young man in Union black who was going to the church. He looked way too young to be with an army, no older than thirteen or fourteen, and he was carrying a tray of food.

"Is that for the werewolves?" Seth asked.

The boy straightened his back, lifted his chin, and gave a stiff nod. "Yes, sir." His voice hadn't even dropped yet.

"Give it to me."

He took the tray and mounted the stairs to the ruined church. The door was barred from the outside. Seth balanced the tray on his shoulder and went inside.

Not much had changed in the church since he was last there with Rylie. The benches had been pushed aside, the holes in the walls had been patched, and a few sleeping bags had been left for the captives. There was a bucket by the door that smelled of human effluence.

"Bekah?" he called, setting the tray on a pew.

Shapes moved in the shadows by the back wall, where there used to be a priest's apartment. Bekah emerged from the doorway. She looked tired and dirty, but uninjured. "Is it feeding time already? I'm having so much fun being imprisoned that the time just flies."

He laughed and offered her a plate. The Union didn't seem to care about the dietary preferences of potential werewolves. They had sent along cornbread, potatoes, and canned beans instead of meat. "Sorry. Are you okay?"

"I'm criminally bored, but they haven't hurt us. Look who I found. Hey! Stephanie!"

Another woman emerged. She was tall, slender, strawberry blond, and looked much angrier than Bekah. "What's going on? Who is this?"

"This is Rylie's boyfriend," Bekah said. "I told you about him. Seth, this is Scott's daughter. Um, biological daughter. Not adopted, like me and Levi. Stephanie is a doctor and a witch and super cool. She came here to search for me, but the Union grabbed her on the highway up the mountain."

Seth compulsively held out a hand to shake hers, but she stayed back and gave him a cold look that did not seem "super cool" to him.

"I'd say it's a pleasure to meet you, but I'm not feeling polite today. Being locked in this church and forced to relieve myself in a bucket for two days has destroyed my sense of courtesy," Stephanie said.

He shrugged. "It could be worse. I brought food." He offered Stephanie a second plate.

"No, thank you. I've seen what the Union considers food." She scanned him with a critical eye, and it gave him the distinct feeling of being trapped under a microscope. "Don't tell me you listened to their moronic propaganda and enlisted. Bekah didn't say you're stupid."

"I'm not enlisted," Seth said. "Do you know the Union?"

"I've come across them before. Not this unit, but others." She glared around at the church and twisted her mouth. "I can't believe they think I'm a werewolf. For Pete's sake. As if I would ever get myself that dirty."

He rolled his eyes and faced Bekah again. "Who else is here?"

"There are these two Mexicans back in the priest's room. Stephanie knows Spanish, so they've been talking a little." Bekah sat on a pew to eat. "They haven't seen Rylie or Abel. Sorry."

"No. That's good. It's better that way."

Stephanie folded her arms. "I can't stand this place for another day. I'm breaking out—tonight, if I can. What will you do to help us?"

"He doesn't have to do anything," Bekah said before he could respond. "It's dangerous."

"No, I was going to escape too, actually." Seth quickly explained what had happened with his mother to Stephanie, and then described their surveillance in the forest. "They're going to do a sweep and pick up all the humans they can find and put them in the church, too. Everyone dies on the next moon. None of us can be here when that happens."

Bekah picked at the beans, seemingly unable to stomach the cornbread. "What about the mountain? We were called here for a reason, Seth. I can't leave until I know why."

"They'll kill you," he said. "They're going to kill *everyone*."

She grinned. It was less like a smile and more like she bared her teeth in wolfish fear. "They'll have to catch us first. Don't worry about it. We'll sneak out when they leave for that sweep, and there's no reason you should put yourself at risk, too."

"I agree," Stephanie said with a sigh. "Good Lord, I hate these people. You damn kopides are completely incapable of staying out of trouble." She eyeballed Seth. "Are you certain you know what team you're on?"

"I know," he said firmly. He glanced at his watch. He had already been in the church too long to only be dropping off food. "Do you know where the girls' camp is? I want you to meet me there tomorrow, after the sweep. We can figure out what to do from there."

"Okay," Bekah said. "Be careful."

He nodded. "You too."

Leaving the tray of food, Seth stepped outside the church again. The sun had dipped below the trees, but it was still ten times brighter than it was inside the murky ruins.

Yasir stood at the bottom of the stairs with a shotgun.

"What were you doing in there?" he asked.

Seth gave a casual shrug. "I was dropping off food."

"You weren't assigned to do that."

"I wasn't assigned to do anything. I'm not a member of your team. I wanted to see how Bekah's doing."

It didn't look like the answer satisfied him, but Yasir only nodded. "Follow me."

They walked through the camp together. In the time that he'd been inside the church, the units had jumped into motion. The men who had been eating were gearing up. Those who had been training were assembled by the main tent.

"What's going on?" Seth asked when Yasir stopped to let a line of men march past.

"The team's mobilizing."

"For the sweep?"

He nodded. "It will be dangerous, you know. Sometimes, a werewolf that feels threatened will spontaneously shift. They're wild between moons. Men could get hurt." Yasir cast a sideways look at him. "The Union always needs good doctors."

Seth blinked. "What are you saying?"

"If you wanted enlist, the Union could send you to medical school. Full ride scholarship to any university you want, and an apprenticeship on the front lines of our war against evil. Nobody else could give you that."

He gaped, unable to find words.

The line of men passed them, and Yasir continued to the supply tent.

"Listen to me, kid. The Union's a good team to be on. A good guy like you deserves a good team. The *right* team." It was like he had heard Seth's conversation with Bekah inside the church.

He struggled not to react. "Is that an invitation?"

"Definitely. I don't need an answer now. Just... mull on it."

Half of the camp was lined up to get their guns, including Stripes and Jakob. Yasir marched Seth straight past them.

The number of weapons inside the tent was staggering. Seth missed his rifle, which had been lost with the Chevelle, but the one that Yasir handed to him was a Lamborghini in comparison. His excitement waned when he saw that it was loaded with silver bullets.

"A group of confirmed werewolves have been located," Yasir explained. "We caught a fight on camera. One of them even changed in the middle of the day. So we have all the proof we need to exterminate them."

The commander left a pause after that, like he was waiting to see how Seth would react.

He had a terrible feeling he knew who had been fighting by the cabins.

It took all his strength to make himself copy Stripes's bored expression. If the Union was hunting Rylie and Abel that night, Seth wasn't going to get left behind.

"Okay," he said with forced calm. "When do we leave?"

Fifteen

Pack

Rylie took Toshiko and the red-haired werewolf, who asked to be called Trick, to the beach before going back to camp for more blankets and pillows. She grabbed extra cans of food while she was at it, too. If she was going to start collecting werewolves, she would need a lot more of everything.

When she returned to the beach, she found Trick with a massive black eye.

"Your friend is back," he said, washing blood off his cheek in the lake. The bruise was already healing, but it looked like his pride was seriously damaged.

She had to laugh. "Lost that fight, too?"

"The man's a beast! You said 'friend,' and I thought it would be another cute girl!"

"Abel's not that much of a beast," she said, feeling strangely defensive, even though she had called him worse names many times. "Just don't challenge him for territory. He doesn't like it very much."

"I see that," Trick said, splashing more water on his face.

Rylie waded through the lake to drop blankets off with Toshiko. The new wolves had taken one of the bigger caves on the edge, and the woman was already curled up on the sand and totally unconscious. Rylie set everything down without disturbing her and paddled to her cave.

Abel was waiting for her. He had the duffel bag.

"I found people," she started to say, but then he turned around and she saw that he held the box of letters in his hand.

Her amusement at Trick's black eye vanished in an instant. She could tell by the way that Abel approached that he had found the stolen gun.

He lifted it between them. "What is this?" he asked, eyes bright with anger.

"Those are my letters," she said. Her voice was very small.

He flung the box to the rocks. The wood cracked at the corners and the lid flew open. All the letters spilled out, and so did the gun. It slid to a stop with its end pointing at her feet. Her cheeks burned. She bit her lower lip and focused on her toes in the sand so she wouldn't have to see Abel's fury.

His low growl was almost worse than being yelled at. "For the last few days I've been asking myself, what's that silver smell? I mean, we don't have anything silver. And you know, I still don't have a hang of the werewolf senses. There are a lot of scents I don't understand yet. So when I found that box in the car and I smelled the silver…"

Her fists trembled at her sides, but she didn't look up. "You shouldn't have opened that. It's my private box."

Abel grabbed the pistol and shoved it in her face. She took a reflexive step back. "And this is my gun! What the hell are you doing with my gun, Rylie?"

The wolf inside of her responded to his heat in kind. It fed off the humiliation and grew to occupy every empty space in her skull. She snapped.

"It's for me!" she yelled.

His hand wavered. "You were going to use this… on yourself?"

Rylie made herself meet his gaze, and she let all of the wolf's rage, all the pain, show in her gold-flecked eyes. "I've killed people, Abel. And that's not the worst part. The worst part is that I don't even remember it. I don't know what I did, or who I killed, or if they... if they suffered." Her voice hitched. "I'm a monster."

"So this is your answer?" Abel unloaded the gun and shook the bullet in her face. The wolf wanted to bite his hand off.

"It's my choice," she said. Her eyes burned with tears.

"That's not a choice. That's a copout! What's wrong with you, Rylie?"

"What's wrong with me? I got bitten by a werewolf, that's what's wrong with me. I can't control when I change, and when I do, it hurts. It *hurts*, Abel."

"Yeah, it hurts," he said. His lip was curled with anger and the tendons in his neck were rigid. "But you know what? You deal with it. That's what you do. You don't go and shoot yourself!"

She reached for the bullet in his hand, but Abel was too fast. He stepped out of her reach and threw it with all of his strength. It plunked into the lake and sank.

"Hey!" she protested.

Abel he spread his fingers wide to show that his skin had blistered where he held the bullet. "You see what that does? You want that in your skull?"

Her jaw ached. She pressed her hands against her temples. "It's better than having this *thing* inside of me!"

"You really think it's better to be dead?"

"Yes!"

Abel's eyes widened. His mouth moved, but no response came out, like the ability to speak had fled from him. He paced to the front of the cave and then back again, weighing the gun in his hand as he glared at her. Finally, he seemed to come to a silent decision.

He shoved the pistol into the waistband of his jeans.

"What are you doing?" Rylie asked.

"This is my gun. I'm taking it back."

"But I need it."

Abel grabbed her shoulders in both of his huge hands and forced her to face him. The span of his fingers almost wrapped all the way around her arms. "What would Seth say if he knew what you were thinking? What do you think he would do if you killed yourself?"

The mention of his name put her over the edge, and once the tears started flowing, it was like breaking open a dam. They cascaded down her cheeks and rolled off of her chin. "He wouldn't want me to die. But that's not his choice, Abel. He doesn't have to live with what I've done."

Abel searched her face, confusion and dismay etching his features.

"No," he said forcefully, like it changed anything. "*No*."

"I don't know why you care," Rylie mumbled, hanging her head. "You would have killed me months ago if you could have. And maybe you should have done it. I wouldn't have bitten you, and you wouldn't have turned into this horrible *thing*."

The muscles in his cheek flexed as he clenched his jaw, but the scarred part of his face didn't move at all. Abel gave her a hard shake. "You don't know why I care? You're my pack, Rylie! I need you!" It came out a roar, and his voice was as rough as a wolf's cry.

As though shocked by his own reaction, he dropped her and took a big step back.

Guilt weighed heavily on Rylie. "Abel..."

He didn't look at her. "Killing yourself isn't a choice," he told the wall, more quietly than before, but with no less fury. And then he strode out of the cave, taking the gun and the last of Rylie's choices with him.

•○•

Trick pretended to be busy digging holes in the sand when Rylie finally left the cave. He had probably heard the entire argument, not to mention all the crying she did afterwards. It was too embarrassing to consider.

"Where's Abel?" she asked, scrubbing the tears from her cheeks.

He pointed her up the beach.

Rylie found Abel on the shore a half-mile away. He stared at the moon-dappled surface of the water, and she sat on the log next to him.

He radiated anger and hurt and fury. It was in every tense line of his body, the deep furrow between his eyebrows, and the slant of his eyes. He didn't even acknowledge her when she scooted over to bump her arm against his.

"Hey," she said.

His fists clenched.

Mosquitoes buzzed around them in a cloud without landing. It seemed like even the insects were too afraid to attack them. She nudged a rock with her toe, scooting it through the damp sand to make a divot. The slopping water immediately softened the shape in the sand.

Rylie tilted her head to the side to look up at him. "You wouldn't shoot me. Would you?"

After a long pause, Abel shook his head. It made her sadder than she expected. If he couldn't pull the trigger—Abel, who used to be a scary hunter, who had stalked her and threatened her and tried to ruin her life—then who could do it for her? Who would be there to stop her if she tried to hurt someone?

"But you promised," she whispered.

"I lied."

They shared a long look. Rylie didn't even see the scars anymore. She just saw Abel—who probably had never been as scary as he pretended to be—and all the vulnerability he had been hiding. He said he needed her, and he meant it.

She wanted to be angry with him for lying, but she couldn't find it within herself. She was too tired to be angry anymore.

Rylie rested her head on his shoulder. His body was even hotter than hers. It drove away the late evening chill of spring ice. "I get it," she said.

"Yeah. Sorry."

She didn't bother trying to tell him it was okay. It wasn't. Regret twisted in her heart—not regret at what she had been planning, but regret that he had found out.

There was nothing left to be said about it after that. He had gotten rid of her silver bullet, taken the gun away, and said he wouldn't shoot her. She couldn't trust him to stop her anymore.

"So what's with the new guys?" Abel asked. It was a welcome change of subject.

"I found them in the cabins when I was looking for supplies. They're not even from America, and Trick—that's the red-haired guy—he said that he's run across other groups in the forest. There are werewolves everywhere, from all over the world."

"Yeah. I figured that would happen. But what are those two doing *here*?"

"They were wandering around naked and hungry. What was I supposed to do?"

He rolled his eyes. "You can't pick up werewolves like dumpster kittens."

"Who says?"

"I say. You don't know any of these people. And they're *werewolves*. Soulless murderers. Monsters."

"Like us," she said.

Abel stood up and glowered at her. "Next time you call yourself a monster, I'm done with you. Hear me?"

She was pretty sure he didn't mean it. Rylie rolled her eyes. "Fine."

He jerked his head toward the caves. "We should sleep."

They waded back to the caves and found that Trick and Toshiko weren't alone. Three more people were sitting on the rocks in the shallows. Only one of them was dressed, and all of them were very obviously werewolves. They introduced themselves as Ramona, Hannah, and Peter—a family from Texas.

Rylie stayed back while Abel confronted them. Her wolf was too desperate to attack.

"Where did you come from?" he demanded.

"We ran into them earlier in the week. Thought they might like a place to hide, too, considering the odd things that have been happening lately," Trick said with a shrug. "It's not a problem, is it? It's not like you own the caves."

"Dumpster kittens," Abel muttered. Louder, he said, "I don't care. Okay? But stay out of *my* cave."

He sloshed through the water to the spot that he and Rylie had claimed for themselves. She gave Trick a sheepish smile before following.

She had gotten so used to having other werewolves around at the sanctuary that she settled down pretty quickly, despite the foreign smells. In fact, she almost felt a little safer knowing they were out there. But guilt weighed too heavily for her to sleep. She couldn't stop thinking about Abel's fingers blistered by the silver bullet.

She pulled the scratchy wool blanket up to her chin, closed her eyes, and tried to sleep.

Something moved in the cave. She peeked through a slitted eye. Abel sat over her, elbows on his knees, and a frown twisting his mouth. She shut her eyes again and pretended to be asleep.

Eventually—maybe minutes later, maybe hours—she sank into unconsciousness.

And Abel kept watching.

Sixteen

Extermination

Rylie woke up to find Abel missing and the crescent moon high overhead, still hours away from sunrise. Pushing back her blankets, she waded ankle-deep into the surf to peer around the side of the rocks. Someone was sitting on the beach, but it was too dark to make out their features.

"Abel?" she whispered. He didn't respond.

When she reached his side, she realized that it was Trick stretched out on his back. He pillowed his head on his arms to watch the moon. He smiled when he saw her.

"Trouble sleeping?"

She sat next to him. "A little bit."

"Dreaming of the mountain?"

"Actually, no. I think…" She took a deep breath. "It sounds silly, but I think my wolf is happy I'm here. So I don't *need* the dreams anymore."

"Same here," Trick said, scratching his chin through the mess of his beard. "I can still feel it calling, though."

She felt the same, but it was too creepy to admit aloud. "Did you see where Abel went?"

"Nah. He wandered off, but I avoided him. I don't need another black eye."

"I tried to bite your arm off. Why aren't you avoiding me?"

He winked. "You're much cuter than he is."

Rylie rolled her eyes.

"Where's everyone else? Toshiko and the new guys?"

"They're all sleeping in the caves. Another two wandered in after you went to bed. Hope you don't mind."

Rylie could already hear Abel's reaction. *Dumpster kittens.* She tried not to smile.

"Well, I don't care. We'll just have to get more blankets tomorrow. There's tons of them back at camp. Do you know any of the people who came in this afternoon?"

"No. They're all perfect strangers to me. And I wouldn't mind if it stayed that way, to be frank," Trick said. "I'd like to never see any of your smiling faces again, once the mystic hootenanny is over."

"Okay. Fine. I was only trying to make conversation."

Rylie started to stand, but he flicked sand at her. "Don't make me sit out here on my own. Sit back down. Tell me how you can change into a werewolf in the middle of the day. Bet that's wicked good craic."

"It's silver poisoning," she said. She wiggled her toes into the cool sand. "It's not that interesting. I promise. I can't even control it."

"How'd you go and get silver poisoning?"

Abel's mom had shot her and left silver-injected meat for her to find at school. It was the stuff of nightmares, and very firmly on the list of "creepy subjects she didn't want to talk about." So she shrugged. "That's not an interesting story, either."

Trick laughed. "You're killing me."

"If you're bored, why don't you tell me how you got bitten? I'm sure it's a lot more interesting than my story."

"Oh, aye, it's a good one," he said. "It's a steamy tale of unrequited love, excellent beer, and an accidental nip from my ex-girlfriend, who was a dog in more ways than one." Rylie giggled, and he nudged her knee. "See? I told you it's good."

"It sounds very good. I don't know if—"

A distant popping noise cut her off. It cracked through the air and echoed off of the trees. Trick sat up, his long hair crusty with sand.

"What was that?" he asked.

"I don't know," Rylie said after a moment's pause. The sound didn't repeat. "It kind of sounded like fireworks or something."

And then it popped again.

A moment later, someone screamed.

"Gunfire," Trick said. "That's gunfire, isn't it?"

And then a group of men burst from the trees. Three of them. They were dressed in black and blended in with the night, and the smell of gun lubricant was so strong that it came off of them in waves.

The men were shouting.

"On your knees! Hands over your head!"

Rylie was so shocked that she fell over instead of obeying, or better yet, trying to run.

But Trick didn't take it nearly as well.

He got to his feet with a wolfish howl that echoed through the night and dived for the nearest man. They seemed to be ready for his attack. One of them slammed the butt of his gun into Trick's stomach and knocked the wind out of him.

Another of them put him in a headlock. The third said, "Light them up."

They hauled Rylie onto her knees. Flashlights clicked on. They aimed them at Trick's face and held a photo next to his chin.

He snarled and twisted, but the man holding him had a great grip. Veins bulged in his arm as he struggled to hold Trick's head steady. One of the other guys had to jump on his legs to keep him from breaking free.

"Yep," said the one left standing. "This is the one that healed really fast after the fight. Get him."

In the past few months, Rylie had been too close to way too many firing guns for her comfort. Guns were a pretty normal part of life on a ranch—shooting coyotes, putting animals out of their misery, filling wrecked cars with holes for fun—but they had fired at her more than once. It was an experience she never wanted to repeat, but she was getting used to them.

It didn't make it less surprising when one of the men pressed his gun to the back of Trick's skull and fired.

The shot exploded through the night air.

Rylie's hands flew to her mouth as she screamed. Even though it was too dark to see the damage, she saw the way he slumped and smelled the gunpowder and blood.

When Trick hit the sand, he didn't move again.

"Grab his teeth, identify the girl, and let's get going," said a man in black. "There's tons of them out there. They're scattering like rats."

A hand fisted in Rylie's hair and jerked her head back. She cried out as they shone the bright light in her face like they had with Trick. She blinked rapidly. Her eyes streamed, and it wasn't just from the burn of the light.

They killed Trick.

A responding thought rose inside of her: *They're killing my pack.*

"Well, look at that. She matches the picture," her captor said. "This is the wolf that fought the red-haired guy. Makes our job easy, doesn't it?"

"Yeah, go ahead and shoot her."

Rylie saw the shadow of the gun turning toward her like it was in slow-motion, and her mind replayed the horrible sight of Trick's death in her mind a hundred times in a single heartbeat. The ear-shattering *bang.* The slump of his body.

For the first time, she deliberately turned inward, focusing on the ache in her jaw and the itch in her nails, and she cried out to her inner wolf: *Help me!*

The change came upon her faster than ever before.

The wolf crested and crashed like an ocean wave, and she barely had time to see the fine spray of blood as her claws erupted.

Someone yelled. "Watch out!"

Rylie twisted and jabbed her entire hand upward. Her fingers connected with something soft. The person with the gun screamed and fell.

She leaped to her feet and ran.

But she hadn't just gotten claws. The wolf had started to take over the rest of her body, too, which meant her bones creaked and groaned as they changed length. Her kneecaps made strange popping noises with every step.

Gunshots rang out behind her and hit the sand near her feet. They only barely missed. She tried to pick up speed, but her feet were too clumsy. She tripped a few yards down the beach.

"Get her!"

"She got me! I'm bleeding!"

"Just shoot—"

The third voice cut off with a strangled yell.

Rylie stopped struggling to get up again and turned. Someone new had pinned one of the men to the ground and ripped the rifle from his hands. He turned it around, fired twice at the others, and then whipped it across the face of the man beneath him.

Abel might not have been able to turn into a wolf on command, but he was just as terrifying in human form.

She was so happy to see him she could have cried. But wolves didn't have tear ducts.

"Help me!" she yelled with a distorted, growling voice.

The two men on their feet fled for the forest, and Abel fired after them as he hurried to Rylie's side. He ran out of bullets, flung the rifle aside, and grabbed her arm.

"Did they hurt you?" he asked, searching her shifting face with his eyes.

"They killed Trick," she groaned. Her ribs were shifting inside her body, growing to make room for her changing organs, and they rippled along her sides. "Abel, I think I'm about to turn—"

"Don't," he said shortly.

Abel hauled Rylie to her feet, hugged her to his broad chest, and half-carried her to the nearest rocks. Flashlights danced in the shadows of the trees. Men shouted as they searched.

"I don't think I can stop it, Abel!"

He pulled her into hiding beneath a rock and pinned her to the boulder. The moonlight glinted off the whites of his eyes. "If you change right now, I will club you like a baby seal," Abel said. "I'm completely serious. Look at me, Rylie."

The weird turn of phrase pierced through the wolf's fury. Rylie loved seals. They were one of the many reasons she had decided to be a vegetarian and avoid animal products.

"That's the worst euphemism I've ever heard," she whimpered.

He nodded. "Yeah. Right. It *is* horrible. And I'll do it. Baby seals."

For a moment, she was suspended in that mental place between girl and wolf. But Abel's glare and the press of his hands slowly dragged her back to her human side. She stopped fighting. Her body sagged in his grip.

"You're a really terrible person," Rylie said. "Seals are such nice animals."

He didn't let go of her. "You good?"

She nodded.

Abel dropped his hands and peered around the side of the rocks. The popping had stopped, but the screaming hadn't.

Things in the forest shifted and cracked like a stampede through the underbrush. The flashlights were on the wrong side of the beach, but they were still hunting for wolves. Hunting for *her*.

"They have my picture," she said.

"Shut up and don't think about it. Stick close. We've got to move."

He drew the gun from the small of his back and eased around the corner. Rylie bit back her retort at being told to shut up and followed.

Abel started to run up the path away from the hunters. She grabbed his wrist. "Wait! What about the other werewolves?"

"Not my pack, not my problem," he said.

"But they need help!"

He stopped and grabbed her elbow. "We can't help them if we're dead. You said it yourself: they have *your* picture, Rylie. They want to kill *you*. We have to run tonight. We can help anyone who's left tomorrow. Okay?"

She bit her bottom lip and gazed at the lights up on the beach. The fear was nauseating. She couldn't stand the idea of having one of those guns pointed at her again.

Rylie wasn't proud of herself for it, but she nodded.

Abel dragged her off. "You scared the crap out of me, Rylie. I saw Trick, and I thought they killed you."

"They almost did." She hurried to keep up with him, but the wolf didn't need her help to navigate the dense forests of the night. It had a perfect mental map of where she was going, which left her mind free to replay Trick's collapse again and again. "Oh my God, Abel. They killed him. They shot him like... like it was nothing."

He didn't look at her or say anything in return, but his hand shifted from her elbow to her hand. She was too stunned to be comforted.

Abel paused on top of a ridge looking down at the lake, staying low so that the floodlights sweeping through the forest wouldn't fall on them. "We need somewhere to hide," he muttered without releasing Rylie's hand. He drummed the pistol against his knee. "We need a den."

The breeze shifted. An odd smell caught Rylie's nose.

She tore her gaze from the beach to look up the mountain.

Someone was watching them from the cliff above.

It was too dark to make out any features with her eyes, but she smelled oil and gunpowder and leather. For a hopeful instant, she thought it might be Seth. But the shape was too slender, and the smell was sour, like everything about Seth gone wrong. Rylie narrowed her eyes. It looked like a woman's face.

No way.

"Abel," she whispered, tugging on his arm. "Abel, look—"

He followed her pointing finger, but the woman had disappeared. "What?"

"Oh. I guess... never mind."

Rylie didn't want to say what she was thinking. Not if there was any chance it might not be true. But a deep, primal fear had filled her at the smell of that woman, and the wolf was almost certain that it had been Eleanor watching.

"Let's move," Abel said.

They found a dense thicket of trees a mile away, where they could hear the shooting without being seen, and hid underneath a felled log. It seemed like the gunshots and screaming went on for hours.

After that, the night was filled with the silence of death.

•○•

In all the years Seth had spent hunting werewolves, facing them down had always been harrowing. He walked the line between being the hunter and the hunted. Even though he was better armed and had been trained by his family, it was still a fair fight.

But the Union assault on werewolves hadn't been a fight.

It was a massacre.

Seth had gone all night without firing a single shot. He followed a group that combed the cabins, certain that it was where Rylie would hide, but the camp had been empty. He missed all the action. And when dawn broke over the beach, Seth had to help drag the bodies into rows by the water so he could see for himself.

The men had killed three werewolves and trapped two others to take back to the church. A heavyset woman and middle-aged man were hogtied by the rocks, where the pictures the Union used to identify the victims were posted on a log nearby. Three of them were crossed out with red marker. He realized with a sickening jolt that the other two were photos of Rylie and Abel from a surveillance camera. His brother had grown a goatee. Seth would have to pick on him for that later.

So they were alive, but they were marked.

"Want to help me pull teeth?" Stripes asked cheerfully when he noticed Seth nearby.

"No," he said, feeling faint. "I'm going to sit down."

He slumped to a log and cradled his head in his hands. Seth watched as a couple of Union men carried more bodies out of the forest. That increased the number of dead to six. How many families would grieve for the loved ones who never came home?

Yasir tracked down Seth a few minutes later. "How's it going?" asked the commander.

"Great," Seth said dully. "Just great."

"Walk with me."

They went to the edge of the forest, away from the Union members picking through the bodies. Everyone was examining dead werewolves or ripping teeth out of skulls, so he was happy to get away from them. He felt like a ghost drifting across the beach.

The commander stopped by the trees.

"We didn't kill those last three," Yasir said.

"What?"

"You heard me. We didn't kill those last three. Someone found them shot and stabbed with silver behind the camp. We don't even have verification that they're werewolves."

There was a certain weight to his gaze that spoke volumes. Seth sucked in a hard breath. If they hadn't been killed by the Union, then who else would have done it? Territory fights between werewolves wouldn't have ended with a gunshot.

Eleanor was on the hunt.

Yasir nodded when he saw realization dawn in Seth's eyes, and he held out the shotgun.

"What am I supposed to do with that?"

"Take it," Yasir said. Slowly, he obeyed. He checked the chamber. It was loaded with normal ammunition. "Look, kid, I know your allegiance. You said your brother's a werewolf. Your girlfriend's a werewolf. You went into the church to check on the werewolf girl. And you didn't take a single shot last night."

"But I've killed werewolves before. Probably more than anybody else here."

"I don't want you with us anymore."

"Does that mean I'm not welcome to join the Union now?"

"No, you can come find me if you decide to join the right team. The Union would be happy to have you, and I'll send you to training immediately. But you can't be *here*. Not this week. Not until the werewolves are dead."

Seth almost turned and left right at that moment, but he hesitated. He liked Yasir too much to go without trying to change his mind. "They aren't always monsters, you know. Some of them are bad, but they don't lose their souls when they get bitten, no matter what my dad's book says."

"Yeah. I know."

He almost dropped his shotgun. "You already know?"

"Doesn't change the fact that they're dangerous. Werewolves are a pandemic waiting to happen, and we can't let them spread." The commander patted his shoulder. "Sorry, kid. But hear this: just because the werewolves are still human doesn't mean they can't be monsters, too." He waved at the forest. "Move it. If I come across you again, we're going to be enemies, so you might want to leave the forest. But if you stay, you can make yourself useful."

"How?"

He put his hand over Seth's on the gun. His skin was rough and his grip was heavy. "Eleanor is still out there somewhere. Find her and get rid of her," Yasir said. "She's the biggest monster of them all."

Seventeen

Licking Wounds

Rylie woke up curled into a stiff ball with a spider crawling down her shoulder. She gasped and flung it away.

For about three blessed seconds, having a big furry bug climbing on her was the biggest problem in the world. But when the spider was gone and she finished waking up, she was still hidden under a log with Abel. She sat up as much as she could in the cramped space and brushed off her arms to chase away the ghost of eight spindly legs on her skin.

Rylie had spent the night reclined against Abel's shoulder, and he was still asleep. His long legs were squeezed into a crevice, which put his knees by his ears. He looked even more uncomfortable than she had been. Even in sleep, there was a gun hanging from his fingers.

Crawling to the edge of the log, Rylie stuck her head out into the forest to sniff the air.

The sun was shining and everything glistened with dew. Hunters had passed sometime in the night, and she could see where their boots left impressions in the mud. The odors were old and stale, and there was no hint of Eleanor's aroma. She hadn't followed them.

"Abel," she whispered. "Wake up."

His eyes flew open. "What time is it?" he groaned, rubbing one big hand down his face.

"I don't know, but the sun is up, and we're not dead yet."

He groaned as he dislodged himself from his uncomfortable position at the back of the log. His knees audibly popped when he stretched out his legs. "Oh, man. Being dead wouldn't hurt so much. Let me out."

She scooted back, and Abel crawled after her. He hadn't managed to acquire any wolfish grace since transforming. He was too tall and broad to move easily on his hands and knees.

He took a sniff before standing up. "Don't relax yet," he warned. "They might still be out there."

He didn't have to tell her that. Rylie didn't think she would ever relax again—not after what they did to poor Trick. Abel set off up the slope, interrupting her slide into miserable depression.

"Where are you going?" she asked.

"I'm sick of this damn mountain," he said. "I'm going to the top to look for answers. That's where the dream kept showing me."

"What about the other wolves?"

"I don't know, what about them?"

"We have to see if they're okay. What if someone's injured? What if they need our help?" Rylie asked.

He rolled his eyes. "Are you kidding?"

She folded her arms and lifted her chin. "No. You can run off to the mountain if you like, but I'm going back to the beach."

"And what happens if you get there and the hunters are still around?"

"Then I stay out of the way," she said.

"We're not going to the beach so that you can play out some hero fantasy. I'm not suicidal." She opened her mouth to argue, but he jabbed a finger at her chest. "And you're not allowed to be suicidal, either! I promised to look after you, so you're coming with me."

Rylie huffed. Abel was a master of never letting an argument drop. If she tried to hash it out with him, they could be there until sunset fell again. "I'm going," she said.

She marched down the slope in bare feet, following the smell of water and sand and blood.

Abel swore loudly and ran after her.

The beach was empty, but there were puddles of blood and body-sized indentations that were slowly being washed away by the surf. Rylie stared at the dents in the sand. One of them still smelled like Trick. The others were unfamiliar, so Toshiko was probably okay. But their caves definitely weren't safe anymore.

Abel sloshed into the water and returned a few minutes later with their belongings packed into the duffel bag again. He pulled the strap across his chest.

"We're going to have to keep moving," he said. "Nobody is here."

"They have to be close. Look." Rylie counted out the shapes in the sand. "Six people died, but there are tons more of us in the forest."

"So maybe the Union killed them somewhere else. Who cares?"

She stood in front of him and blocked his path to leave. She was much smaller than Abel in every way, but she was an older werewolf by a few months, and her wolf liked to think it was his superior. "I care."

"For a smart girl, you can be really stupid."

He was totally baiting her, but she ignored it for once. Rylie took his hand. "What if Seth was hurt out there somewhere? Wouldn't you want someone to find him, too?"

"Seth *is* out there somewhere. But he's with the guys who have guns," he reminded her. When she didn't waver, his cynical glare went soft. "Fine. Whatever. I don't care. Let's check out the camp. Five minutes, then we're going. Okay?"

"Okay."

They walked together through Camp Silver Brook. When Rylie had searched it before, it had been a like a haunting, empty museum of the place she had spent her last summer. After the hunters blew through it, it looked like a war zone instead. They had shattered windows, kicked in doors, knocked over benches, and left bullet holes in the walls.

Rylie found more blood in the dirt. It was almost drying. Whatever had happened, nobody had been there for hours.

She sniffed around, and she stitched together an image of the rampage from the previous night. Werewolves had run through in human form. Some of them had been poisoned with silver and changed. A few people had definitely died. And a *lot* of guns had been discharged.

"Maybe everyone really is dead," she said when they reached the cabins of Group D. The idea upset her a lot more than she expected.

Abel didn't pick on her, for once. "Hold this." He shoved the duffel bag into her arms. "Stay here, and don't touch my guns. I'll be back in a minute."

"Where are you going?"

He dug his pistol out of one of the pockets. "I said, I'll be back in a minute."

Abel jogged into the forest.

Rylie dropped the duffel bag and sat down next to what used to be a campfire. What had she been hoping to find when she returned to camp? Did she think there would be a pack waiting for her?

Footsteps crunched on the dirt behind her.

She froze. Trick's death flooded her mind again—the *bang*, the slump, her scream—and it took all her strength not to wolf out in an instant.

Rylie looked over her shoulder.

A girl her age with long, honey-blond curls stepped into the clearing. Her hooked nose offset a brilliant smile with perfect white teeth. A white blanket was wrapped around her like a toga, and even though her legs and feet were dirty, she looked healthy.

Rylie's mouth dropped open. She stood. "Bekah!"

"Rylie!"

They ran to each other and hugged. Rylie's inner wolf would have purred, if such a thing were possible. Everything about Bekah's smell said *pack*—the scent of warm California sunshine, the familiar sweat on her skin, and even Stephanie's perfume, which Rylie had often scented on Scott.

"Are you okay? Everyone was so worried about you!"

"I'm fine," Bekah said. "A little embarrassed that I ran away, you know? But fine. Look at you! Does this mean everyone is here? Where are Scott and Levi?" Before Rylie could respond, the other girl kept talking at about a million miles a second. "I have Stephanie! She came looking for me and we both got captured! But oh my gosh, Seth is going to be so happy to see you! He's supposed to meet me here."

"Wait, slow down," Rylie said. "You were caught by people? Stephanie is here? You saw Seth?"

As if summoned by the sound of her name, Stephanie Whyte marched into the clearing between the cabins. Rylie had never seen her looking anything less than perfectly-coiffed and professional, but her hair had fallen from its severe bun, and she was just as dirty as Bekah. "Oh good. It's you. I thought we would have to search for days to find everyone. Of course, I also seem to remember Scott telling you to stay back at the sanctuary."

"Sorry," Rylie said, giving a sheepish smile.

The doctor cracked a smile in return. "But it's good to see that you're in good shape."

"You too. What's going on?"

Bekah gave her a quick rundown of hitching a ride out to Gray Mountain, getting caught by a group calling themselves "the Union," and why Seth was with them. "But he's only doing it so he can find you," she added immediately.

Rylie's heart warmed. "Are you sure?"

"Yeah." Bekah faltered. "Pretty sure. I mean, it's Seth. He loves you. This Union, though, they're nuts. And they had Seth's mom."

And all the warmth disappeared in an instant.

So she *had* seen Eleanor.

Abel returned to the clearing, his gun jammed in his belt and two big hunks of black plastic in his hands. "Hey, Bekah," he said, barely glancing at her. "Check this out, Rylie."

She rolled her eyes and took one of the plastic pieces from him. It looked like some kind of camera. Wires stuck out of its body, and there were broken pieces of a glass lens. "Where did you find this?"

"I saw sunlight reflecting off of it in the trees. They're everywhere, once you know what to look for. I've shot down five of them already." Abel turned the other piece over to show her a stamp that said "UKA" with a logo of a circle bisected by an arrow. "This one's a motion detector or something. We're being watched."

"We certainly are," Stephanie said. "The Union has surveillance throughout the entire forest. Fortunately, if I can reach Scott, he should have the van. We could all leave before this turns into more of a massacre."

"I don't have a phone," Rylie said. "And there are no towns for miles."

"My cell phone is at the Union compound. I didn't get a chance to find it before Bekah and I sneaked out last night. Escape was our priority."

"I'll get it," Abel said.

"Don't be stupid. There are a dozen armed men waiting there, and almost as many witches trained in some form of offensive magic. You would die. If we want to contact Scott, we need a better plan than that." Stephanie drummed her fingers on her chin. "Does anyone have a quartz crystal? I could perform a communication ritual."

Abel rolled his eyes. "Yeah, let me go grab mine. This is moronic," he said.

Stephanie glared. "If you have a better plan that doesn't involve getting shot, I would love to hear it."

"We attack them," Rylie said. Everyone looked at her. She shrugged. "We've got three werewolves here. We can move really fast. We might not be able to win, but we could distract them and give you enough time to sneak in for your phone, Stephanie."

The doctor considered Rylie's suggestion. "It sounds like a terrible idea…"

"That's because it is," Abel said.

"…but a less forward approach might have merit."

He stepped up to argue, but he was cut off by a newcomer bursting into the clearing. Toshiko rushed to Rylie and collapsed at her feet.

For a heartbeat, she was just relieved to see Toshiko was alive, but then she noticed that all of the dark patches on her skin weren't mud. A lot of it was blood, too.

"Are you okay?" she asked, even though she knew there was no way Toshiko would understand.

She responded and pointed to the forest. Rylie didn't understand a single word, but the desperation on her face was clear. "Someone must be injured," Stephanie said. "Take us there."

When Toshiko only stared, Rylie nudged her. "Let's go."

They trooped through the trees. They didn't have to hike far. The werewolves had hidden out underneath a craggy rock face to the north, closer to the peak. There were four people waiting. Rylie didn't recognize a single face, which meant the Texan family must have been captured or killed. Two of them were naked, probably having lost their clothes during the last transformation, and both were covered in as much blood as Toshiko. They were groaning on the ground.

"What's wrong?" Rylie asked when Toshiko dragged her to the prone bodies.

"They got shot," said a man crouched in the corner. The two on the ground looked like they were in too much pain to be coherent. "What's going on here? Why are people hunting us? How did we get to this mountain?"

"It's okay, we have a doctor," she said, hoping that would be reassuring enough to calm those wide, frenzied eyes. It was easier than trying to answer the questions.

"Move. Let me see," Stephanie said, brushing past Rylie to crouch by the injured werewolves. She examined the wounds with gentle, confident fingers. "There are bullet fragments in the wounds. That's why they're not healing. I'll need supplies. Scissors, alcohol if possible, some gauze—"

"There's an infirmary at camp," Rylie said.

Bekah leaped to her feet. "I'll see what I can find."

Rylie followed the other girl before Abel could try to stop her. She didn't want to be around all those strange werewolves. Even though her own beast was quiet after the horrors of the night, she didn't trust it not to try to attack the weak ones when it had a chance.

They ran down the trail with long, loping strides and pumping fists. Normal wolves could cover a hundred miles in a day when they were determined. Werewolves were even faster.

When the wind blew in Rylie's face, she picked up that gunpowder and leather smell again. She hesitated at a fork in the trail.

"What's wrong?" Bekah asked.

Rylie spun, searching the trees with her eyes for Eleanor. Her heart hammered as her adrenaline spiked.

But it wasn't Eleanor's smell she'd caught on the breeze.

Higher on the mountain and across the river, Rylie saw a black shape standing atop the rocks. She closed her eyes and took another deep breath.

It was Seth. She was sure of it.

He had stopped moving, and she thought he was looking in her direction. He must have spotted her, too.

She lifted her hand and gave a small wave.

He waved back. Her heart skipped a beat.

The other girl searched, but she didn't see what Rylie saw. She wasn't magnetically drawn to Seth like that.

"Okay, listen to me, Bekah. The nurse's station isn't far from the office," Rylie said. "Kind of between the mess hall and the office. It's easy to find. You can grab a laundry bag and take a bunch of supplies back to Stephanie."

"Aren't you coming?"

"I have to do something," she said. "I'll be back soon. I promise."

Bekah nodded. "Okay. Be careful."

She left, and Rylie saw Seth point toward camp before jumping down the back of the rocks where she couldn't see him.

He wanted to meet her at the camp. She knew she shouldn't have been so excited, not when Abel claimed that Seth had turned on them. But realizing she was about to see him turned off her common sense.

After all those letters, and trying desperately to ignore his phone calls, she was going to see him again.

Rylie didn't care if Seth was with the hunters or not. She had to meet him.

Eighteen

The Cabin

Rylie knew instinctively that Seth would go to the cabin where she had stayed the summer before. It was far enough from the rest of the camp that the Union had missed it on their rampage, and the windows were intact. She had to break the handle to open the door.

Stepping inside was like time traveling. Everything about that summer returned to her all at once: avoiding everybody for her first two weeks at camp, the way the counselors watched her, creek walking and archery and arts and stupid crafts. She even remembered stealing the counselor's car to go to the boys' side of the lake, which was pretty laughable now that she knew what she knew. Seth hadn't even been a camper.

But beyond that, her memories were hazy. It was like the wolf had eaten holes in her brain.

She turned around to look at the cots with squinted eyes, trying to remember who slept where. Rylie recalled two teenage delinquents staying with her. She couldn't remember what they were in trouble for, or their names. They had survived the attacks, so it didn't really matter. The names that did matter were burned into her mind forever: Louise, Amber, Cassidy, and Jericho. The skeletons in her closet.

Rylie opened the drawer by the nearest cot. It had belonged to the pug-faced girl, who had left things behind in her hurry to escape. She idly picked through it. A paperback with a swooning woman on the cover. A few pens. A dead cell phone. A box of small, crinkly packages. Her cheeks flushed with heat when she realized they were condoms.

Embarrassed, Rylie bumped the drawer shut again and went to her cot. She had left in a hurry, too, so a few of her things were still there. She kind of hoped that one of them would be her journal, but it wasn't there. Instead, there was a stuffed cat with a round body and reaching paws.

"Byron!" she exclaimed, pulling him out of the drawer. Byron the Destructor had been her favorite stuffed animal as a child, and she had taken him everywhere with her for years.

She brushed dust off his bulbous head and pressed her nose to his. Faintly, very faintly, she could smell her own odors on him. At least, she assumed the odors were hers. The person she smelled had used her body wash, and wore hand-me-down clothes from the lost and found, but she didn't smell like a wolf.

Disappointed, Rylie pulled some cobwebs off of his tail and flicked it to the table. She didn't feel nearly as warm toward him as she used to. All those long nights she spent cuddling her stuffed cat were so distant as to be meaningless.

She set him on the pillow as the window creaked open behind her.

Seth climbed in. They stared at each other from across the cabin, breathless and silent.

Rylie wasn't sure if it was a failure of memory or if Seth had changed since the last time they were together, but he looked so much better than she recalled. He was a little taller, and his back was a little straighter. His muscles seemed more developed.

There was something a bit military about him, too. The smell of gunpowder was stronger than ever before. She detected gun oil and synthetic polymers and silver.

It didn't change how she felt. Seth was gorgeous, and just looking at him made her entire body ache. Rylie wanted to run to him and hold him and be held.

She didn't move, and neither did he.

"I knew you would come here," he said.

You're with the hunters.

Rylie bit back the words. Instead of speaking, she only nodded.

Seth gave her a long look. She wondered what he thought of how she had changed. She ran a hand through her hair self-consciously.

He took a step toward her. She stepped back, and he stopped.

"I've been wandering around all day. I found the kayaks." A hint of that crooked smile touched his mouth. "They left the activities shed unlocked. I didn't even have to pick it this time. Do you remember when we went to the boys' side of the lake together?"

She did. She remembered it so clearly that she could almost feel the damp seat under her legs, and the gentle rocking as Seth paddled them across the water.

But her return smile was gone as soon as it began to grow. That girl in the kayak was practically a stranger to her.

He took another step.

"Or when we danced on the beach," he went on. "We weren't supposed to leave the recreation hall, but it was so crowded, and the music was kind of terrible."

She had to crack a smile at that. "I'm a really bad dancer."

"But it was fun."

"Yeah." She didn't move back when he took one more step toward her. They were within arm's reach. His smells were overwhelming. "I didn't think I would ever come back, Seth.

There's a bad memory for every good one. When Louise got killed. Everything about Jericho. That stupid mountain..."

"I've missed you."

Rylie couldn't remember the last time her heart beat. "I've missed you, too."

"Abel?"

"He's around," she said. She wasn't sure if she should tell him about the werewolves hiding under the cliff.

He seemed to sense her trepidation. "Are you okay?"

"No. No, I'm not okay." She took a deep breath. "Abel saw you. In the forest." She didn't mean to let him see how much that hurt her, but there was no hiding it. Her brow furrowed. "*Why?*"

"It isn't what you think."

"How do you know? I don't even know what I think."

"I'm not *with* them. I came here with them because Eleanor made me. She's out there right now."

Having him repeat what Bekah said made her feel a little better. She stared through the window, terrified that she would see eyes staring back, but the only thing on the other side was forest. "What is Eleanor doing here?"

"I don't know what she's doing. I thought she was coming here to work with the other hunters, but she's got something else going on. Some other plan. I'm going to try to find her, but I had to see you first."

She sank onto one of the cots. He knelt in front of her, just inches away, but not touching.

The wolf responded to him like he was a long-lost member of her pack, even though the last time they were alone together, she had attacked him. She hadn't thought it would be possible for the wolf to feel regret, but it did. Or maybe it was getting harder and harder to separate the animal from the girl.

Seth finally rested his hand on hers. Warmth rippled up her shoulders.

"What's wrong?" he asked.

Her eyes blurred. "What's wrong? I'm back in this horrible place with no idea of what's going on. There are hunters out there—*Eleanor* is out there—and even after months of 'rehabilitation,' I still can't think of a good reason I shouldn't give myself to the hunters."

"I can think of a lot of great reasons." He didn't have to actually say any of them aloud. His gaze spoke volumes.

Guilt crept over her. "I've thought about killing myself," Rylie said, picking at her thumbnail. "I've thought about it a lot." She glanced up at him through the sheet of her white-blond hair, but she couldn't make out his expression. She refocused on her hand. "I'm sorry."

Seth cupped her face in both hands. It took her several seconds to get the courage to look up at him.

He wasn't angry at all, like Abel had been. He looked sad.

"I know it hurts," he said.

Something inside of her broke a little, like a crack in a vase. "It hurts so much." A single tear burned a hot path down her cheek. "The things I've done…"

He pulled her down so that their foreheads bumped. It had been so long since she had been touched in such a way that it felt strange and new, like she was being touched for the very first time.

Closing her eyes didn't hold back the tears. They just flowed more freely than ever. She clung to his shoulders like he was the only thing that could keep her on the ground.

They sank to the floor together. He tucked her head under his chin. She listened to his heartbeat and tried to focus on it, wishing she could wrap herself in every one of Seth's sounds and smells and drown in that leathery warmth.

Being held by him didn't make it okay. Nothing would make it okay. But it did remind her of happy things. Not when they met at the camp, but the time they spent together on the ranch. Cold winter mornings fixing fences and feeding chickens. Putting her feet up on his legs while he studied anatomy. Laughing over a pot roast with Gwyn and Abel, like they were a family.

"I don't want to leave you ever again," she said.

"You don't have to."

He kissed her. His mouth was warm and soft and tentative, like he was asking her permission.

For a single, blessed moment, Rylie only felt happy and a little excited. Warmth pooled low in her stomach. But the moment passed, and the wolf stirred in response to her spike in adrenaline.

"We can't do that." Rylie tried to extricate herself from him, but he didn't let go.

"Take deep breaths. Count to ten. Think about human things, like how you didn't have to do finals this year."

The idea of school was ridiculous after everything she had been through. She couldn't even remember what classrooms looked like. The only images she could summon were of icy rivers and cold gray stone.

Seth kissed her again, just as gently as before. Rylie didn't want him to be gentle. She wanted him to hurt her. To be rough, and throw her against the wall, and make her *feel* it. She needed him to take charge and drive away the wolf.

The wolf swelled inside of her. A growl escaped her throat.

"Hey," he murmured, gazing into her eyes. "Don't do that. You can relax."

"I can't help it." She spoke through gritted teeth.

"The sanctuary hasn't helped, has it?"

"All it did was make me miss you," Rylie said. "That's why I didn't call. Or write letters back. But I read every single one, Seth. I've still got all of them."

His response was to dip his head and brush his lips over hers again. When she leaned into him a second time, he didn't pull back. He let her deepen the kiss. Rylie sank into his body.

And her fingernails itched.

She clenched her hands into fists and tried to ignore it. But it only got worse. After a moment, Seth noticed that she had gone stiff. They both looked down. Droplets of blood oozed from her nails where the claws were trying to grow in.

"Tell me what to do," he said. "Tell me how to stop it."

"Distract me. Don't let the wolf take over."

She pressed her body into his as she covered his lips with her own, and he immediately pushed her back onto the floor. His body was heavy on top of hers, almost crushingly so, but it didn't make Rylie feel trapped. It made her feel safe. Secure.

The itching didn't stop, but it didn't grow worse. Seth was in charge. It seemed to make the wolf happy. "Is this okay?" he asked, his hands pressing her wrists into the floor.

Rylie bit her bottom lip. The wolf was content to be under his control. For once, they were both in total agreement with each other. "Just don't stop," she whispered.

And so he didn't.

Nineteen

Reunited

Rylie never had female friends. She usually hung out with guys to avoid girl drama. And the boys were fun, but it meant that she didn't get to talk about relationships very often—though they did talk about sex.

Tyler had the noble distinction of losing his virginity first. Lance, always competitive, followed suit quickly thereafter. Both of them said it was the best thing ever, and that they were totally real men afterward, and high-fived over it. She had rolled her eyes and pretended not to listen.

Now that she had crossed that line, Rylie didn't feel like high-fiving anyone. And she didn't feel like she was an adult all of a sudden, either. In fact, she wasn't even sure if it was the best thing ever—it had started out a lot more awkwardly than she had expected, actually.

But as she stretched out on one of the creaky cots, covered in a scratchy wool blanket as Seth pulled his pants back on, she did feel pretty good about it. And also very shy.

He watched her as he did up his belt again, and there was a knowing heat in his eyes that made her blush and pull the blanket to her chin. "Stop that," she said, letting an giggle slip. Her cheeks were hotter than a campfire.

"Stop what?"

She peeked over the edge of the blanket. "Looking at me."

"Rylie, I just saw all of you." That slanted grin grew. "*Everything*. Don't you think it's a bit late to be shy?"

"Well, you were too busy to stare," she mumbled into the wool. "I can't believe I didn't... you know." She made a fake growling noise, which sounded more like a kitten's purr than her beast's bass hum. "I used to change every time I got one of your letters, and this was a lot more, um, stimulating."

Seth laughed and dropped onto the cot again, framing her head on either side with his forearms. It was harder to tell with his dark skin, but she thought he might be blushing, too. "You didn't change because you're better than this, you can control it, and you're amazing," he said matter-of-factly.

"Shut up. You know I hate it when you get all nice." She swatted at him. "You were getting dressed, weren't you?"

"I can be distracted."

He tried to kiss her again, but she squirmed out of his grip, and he gave up. Seth sat on the edge of the bed to grab his shirt.

When he turned his back, she saw a tattoo on his shoulder. Rylie sat up for a closer look, keeping the blanket hugged around her body, and spread her fingers over the ink. It was a paw print the same size as her hand, encircled by a moon.

That glow flushed through her all over again. "When did you get this?"

"For my eighteenth birthday." Seth shot a crooked smile over his shoulder. "Aunt Gwyn didn't want me to tell you that she paid for it."

Rylie gasped. "She did not."

"Bet you don't know she has a tattoo of a unicorn on her calf, huh?"

"Now you're making stuff up."

Seth laughed, and she couldn't tell if he was picking on her or not. She didn't really care. He wrapped his arms around her and kissed her again, like he had all the time in the world. He seemed to have forgotten all about his shirt.

Then he whipped the blanket off, and she shrieked with laughter as he pounced.

"It's too cold! Give it back!"

"I'll keep you warm," he growled, and she kicked at him playfully as he pressed his body against hers. Even her light-hearted attempts at fending him off were backed by the bruising strength of a werewolf, so Seth chuckled and flopped onto his side. "I give up!"

She flopped onto him and tucked her head into his shoulder. "And I thought I was the animal."

"I learned from the best." He looped his fingers around hers. Silence sank upon them, and the warm peace of being comfortable and cozy was almost too good to break. But after a few moments, Seth craned his neck around to look at her. "We can't stay here for long. People will come looking."

Rylie ran a finger down his bare chest. "I don't see why not."

"Well, we have to eat eventually. And we're still on this stupid mountain with three teams of Union hunters and about fifty werewolves. You won't be much fun to be locked up with in a couple of nights, either."

She sighed. "Yeah. I guess you're right. But Seth?"

"Huh?"

"Can we stay for a few more minutes?"

"Yeah," he said. "We can."

Seth didn't realize he had fallen asleep until a weird noise woke him up.

His eyes popped open. Rylie was curled against his side. She was still totally unconscious, and very quietly snoring, which would have been cute if his heart hadn't been pounding from the adrenaline.

What had disturbed him?

He slipped out of bed, careful not to stir his girlfriend, and went to the window. Rylie rolled over, pressed her face into the lumpy pillow he had vacated, and let out a sigh.

Night had fallen. The moon was quickly becoming full, but he could barely make out the trees beyond the ring of cabins. They were a towering black mass of branches. There wasn't even the faintest breeze to stir them. Clouds blotted out the stars on the east, but they were suspended in the air, like they were waiting for something.

It was quiet. Kind of too quiet.

Rylie's arm flopped to the side, searching for Seth. When she didn't find anything, her eyes cracked open. "What are you doing?" she asked with a sleepy smile.

"I thought I heard something. Stay low."

Her smile was gone immediately. He could tell the wolf's senses were taking over by the calculating look that filled her eyes and the tilt of her head. Seth grabbed his gun and returned to the window, ears perked.

Snap.

The faint sound of a foot pressing against a twig was barely audible through the walls, but it jolted through him as if he had been struck by a sledgehammer.

She moved to his side. "Who is it?" she whispered.

A red dot appeared on the glass. He looked down. It was on Rylie's chest, too, like a glowing freckle. She tried to touch it, but the dot only moved to her hand, lighting up the shadows between her fingers.

Laser sight.

"Get down!"

Seth shoved her to the ground an instant before the shot split the air and shattered the glass. The bullet hit the wall behind them. Rylie screamed.

He took the safety off on his rifle and peeked over the windowsill. Someone was running outside. All he saw was a black shape flashing through the trees. He steadied his aim on the window, tracked their motion for a few seconds, and squeezed the trigger.

Even though Seth hadn't shot the werewolves when Yasir told him to and blamed it on bad aim, he actually had really good aim. Even at night.

Someone cried out. It was a woman's voice.

The runner dropped to the ground, and Seth dropped, too. He pressed his back against the wall.

"What's happening?" Rylie asked. Her voice was surprisingly clear. She hadn't started losing her teeth to fangs again yet. Seth checked her fingers—no claws.

"We're being attacked. We'll have to run."

She nodded, mouth sealed shut in a thin line.

Seth pushed himself up to peek out again, but two more shots blasted through the air and splintered the wood by the window. He threw himself over Rylie to protect her from the falling debris.

"Let's go," he said.

He pulled Rylie to the front door, pausing only to let her scoop her clothes off the ground, and pointed his gun around the corner to pop off a couple of shots without aiming. A responding bullet smacked into the wood deck.

And then another gun began to fire.

He searched for the source of the gunshots, but he couldn't make out any motion. Had Yasir followed him?

Rylie frozen in the middle of wiggling into her shirt. She pointed. "Abel!"

Once she said his name, Seth saw Abel taking cover behind a picnic table. He was shooting blindly into the trees. It seemed to work. The other shooter fired one more time, and then stopped.

Seth stepped down before Rylie, rifle braced against his shoulder as he searched the trees. But Eleanor was gone. There were no more red dots, either.

Rylie bounced down the steps on one foot as she tried to pull on her shorts.

"How did you find us?" she asked, hurrying to Abel's side.

"You've been missing for hours. I followed your trail. Watch out." Abel shoved Rylie behind him and raised the gun to point it at Seth.

He froze in the middle of putting the rifle's strap across his chest.

Rylie grabbed Abel's arm, dragging the pistol down. "Wait!"

He wrenched away from her with a disbelieving look. "Did you seriously just jump me when I had my finger on the trigger? Do you know how easy it would be to accidentally fire?"

"You had your finger on the trigger? Did you actually plan on shooting me?" Seth asked. He lifted both of his hands in a gesture of peace. "Dude, trigger discipline."

"Yeah, I'd shoot you. You're here with hunters. You're here with Mom!" Abel waved the gun at the trees. "That was her, wasn't it? How else did she know where to find Rylie if it wasn't for you?"

"It's not like that, you big dummy," she said, angling to put her body between Seth and Abel. "He only followed the hunters so he could help us. He's still on our side. Okay?"

"Are you willing to risk your life on that?"

"Yes," Rylie said firmly, wrapping her hand around Seth's.

Abel glared at them for a moment longer, and then dropped the gun. "You're hanging out with a bad crowd, bro."

"Not anymore," he said, finally tearing his eyes away from his brother's gun to watch the trees. It was disturbingly quiet again. Midnight was approaching. "But we shouldn't talk here. Let's move."

"Okay." Rylie paused to button up the shorts she had taken from the lost and found before following Abel. She was probably trying to be discreet under her baggy shirt, but Abel noticed anyway. His eyes went from her to Seth, and then his eyebrow lifted.

"Where's your shirt, man?"

Rylie flushed and stared at the sky like it had suddenly become really, really interesting. "I lost it in the cabin," Seth said, trying not to smirk, or look too hard at his girlfriend, or otherwise project "we had awesome sex" vibes all over the place.

But hanging out with werewolves made it really, really hard not to share their private business. Their senses were too keen. Abel's narrowed eyes flicked between both of them, and he could practically see the moment that his brain shifted interpretations of Rylie putting on clothing from "just changed back from werewolf" to "formerly undressed with his half-naked brother."

He leaned over Rylie's shoulder and took a short sniff of the air. She kept staring at the sky. Her face couldn't get any redder.

"Lost your shirt. Uh huh," Abel said. "You lost *something*."

Seth shoved him away from Rylie. "Move it, you ugly maniac. And keep your nose to yourself."

He tried to keep his dignity when he ducked back into the cabin for his shirt.

They were quiet as they headed up the mountain. Rylie and Abel seemed to know where they were going, so Seth took up the rear and watched for any more potential signs of attack. But Abel didn't seem willing to let him out of his sight. He kept a steady gold eye on Seth over his shoulder.

After about an hour, Abel stopped them near a trail.

"I'll go ahead to the rocks and check on them," he said. "Keep your clothes on until I get back."

He vanished.

"Check on who?" Seth asked.

"We've met up with other werewolves. Some of them are injured. I think he wants to make sure that you aren't going to run in and shoot them. Oh, Seth!" Rylie flung her arms around his neck, and he hugged her tightly. "I'm sorry. I don't know why he's being so... I don't know. Weird." Her voice was muffled against his shoulder.

"Ignore him," he said, massaging her back.

"But Abel *knows* about us."

"Yeah. So?"

"So if he knows then—then everyone else will know, too," Rylie said. It was a pretty lame excuse. Seth held her at arm's length and studied her face. Even in the dark, he could see that she was still pink-cheeked and having a hard time looking at him.

"Are you embarrassed because we did it, or because you don't want Abel to know?"

She didn't get an opportunity to respond. Bekah appeared out of the trees.

"You made it!" She hugged Rylie tightly, and then Seth, too. "I was getting worried! Did you run across the hunters again?"

"I think we were attacked by a hunter, yeah. But we're fine. What about everything here? Did Stephanie stitch together the injured wolves?"

Bekah nodded. "They're healing. Come on, everyone's trying to sleep."

She led them back to the hollow under the cliff. The group had expanded again. There were three more people squeezed in the back, and they slept on top of each other in a big pile. Stephanie wasn't sleeping; she was deep in conversation with Abel. Every time Rylie saw her, she seemed to have lost a little more of her composure. Her hair was frazzled and her eyes were shadowed. She still managed to give a thin smile at the sight of Seth.

"Tell her, Rylie," Abel said. "Eleanor's onto us. We have to move *tonight*."

Stephanie huffed. "Not all of these werewolves heal as well as you do. These people have been through a lot, and they're working their way through silver-inflicted injuries. They need rest."

"They'll get enough time to rest if hunters shoot them in the head!"

Seth kneeled by the closest of the injured wolves—a sleeping man with olive skin who looked like he hadn't shaved in a year. He gently moved the gauze to examine the wound. If they had been shot during the beach attack, then Stephanie was right. They were healing too slowly.

"I think she's right," he said. "We should let them sleep it off."

Abel folded his arms. "I didn't ask you."

"I'm really tired," Rylie said helpfully. "Why don't we take turns staying up to watch for hunters? We can leave in the morning."

The vote wasn't in his favor. Abel threw his hands in the air, making a disgusted noise.

"Fine. I'll take first watch."

Twenty

Counterattack

Seth and Abel spent the next morning arguing.

They stood outside the hollow under the cliff and didn't try to keep their voices down. Rylie listened as she helped Toshiko clean up camp. They covered the blood splatters with dirt and picked up their trash so the Union wouldn't know they had slept there.

"We can't stay ahead of the hunters forever. They know too much," Seth said. "Motion trackers, cameras, heat sensors, guns—"

"That's why we should just go to the top of the mountain."

"But they'll expect to find you there. We *have* to go on the offensive." Seth lowered his voice, but Rylie's hearing was good enough that it didn't really matter. "Get Stephanie's phone, call Scott, get the van…"

Abel gave a derisive snort. "I'm not going anywhere until I know why we're here. I need answers!"

"Your answers could get everyone killed. They could get *Rylie* killed," Seth snapped.

Her ears burned. She focused on putting trash in the bag that Toshiko held. The other werewolves were quickly working through their short supply of food, even though trying to choke down cans of vegetables was difficult for werewolves.

They would have to find a new supply of food—preferably meat—and they would have to do it fast.

Stephanie finished working on a patient, who shivered with a werewolf's healing heat. She brushed a thick lock of hair off her forehead with her wrist, since her latex-gloved fingertips were bloody. "You should heal quickly now. Tell me immediately if you notice another bullet fragment emerging." The doctor gestured to Rylie. "Bring me the trash bag."

Rylie took the bag and hurried over, holding it open so the doctor could drop her gloves into it. "Is everyone going to be okay?"

"These ones will be, thanks to my efforts," Stephanie said. She gave Rylie an appraising look. "Let's have a chat." They walked to the back end of the hollow, several feet away from the nearest werewolf. Everyone was starting to move for the entrance. "This is an ugly situation, and it's only going to get uglier. You know that, right? Quite a few people will die."

The memory of Trick sprawling on the sand struck her again anew. Rylie's gut clenched. "I know."

"Seth is right. We *must* get off the mountain. But given the Union's monitoring, it will be more difficult than just calling Scott. We can only fit so many in the van, and anyone left behind would be slaughtered. We must disable the devices at the Union camp first."

"But that's a death trap."

"Yes. It could be, especially for anyone who attempts it as a human. You and Bekah are the only ones who can change between moons, so you'll have to do it, as much as I hate endangering children."

"Abel won't ever let me do that," Rylie whispered.

"We'll separate. Abel will lead everyone up the mountain. You, Bekah, and Seth can splinter off to attack the Union."

"What about you?"

"My skills as a doctor are too valuable to risk losing. Given the lack of alternatives, I'll stay with the group. So what do you think, Rylie?"

She cast her gaze at Abel and Seth at the head of the hollow. It was a steep climb to the surface, so she could only see their legs. Their argument must not have gone well, because they weren't facing each other anymore. "I'll talk to Bekah."

"I was listening," Bekah interrupted. She was seated a few feet away as she tried to eat a can of green beans. "Super hearing, remember? It's a decent plan. Let's do it." She gave a nervous chuckle. "Before I think about it too much."

So it was settled. All the werewolves congregated on the trail outside the rocks. Their numbers had somehow grown again, and there were over a dozen people Rylie didn't recognize. They were a pretty weird mix of ages and nationalities. Many of them didn't even seem to understand English.

Abel climbed on a tall rock to point at the mountain's peak. "We're almost there. Let's finish this!" he shouted.

It was a pretty universal sentiment. People headed up the trail.

Rylie hung back with Bekah to whisper the plan to Seth, who indicated agreement by giving her hand a hard squeeze.

Even though they were turning into a pretty big crowd, it seemed impossible to find a chance to sneak off. The group moved slowly. They had to keep stopping to let the injured people catch up.

And Abel watched Rylie closely. Every time she turned around, she caught sight of his eyes tracking her every motion. It was like getting Seth back only made her more of a target for his watchful stare.

The entire day passed without a chance for her to leave.

"We should go," Bekah whispered to Rylie in the middle of the night. They had stopped to rest in a thicket, and everyone was scattered through the trees. "Now. While everyone's sleeping."

But Abel wasn't sleeping. He sat in a nearby tree, where he had destroyed another tracking device, and watched over everyone.

"Not yet," Rylie whispered back.

She fell asleep before they could sneak out that night. And the next day wasn't good for leaving, either. They had to make supply runs back to Camp Silver Brook in order to feed everyone, and Abel didn't let Rylie or Seth do it.

As they climbed higher on the mountain—so horribly slowly—the air got thinner and colder. Patches of snow started to appear. The plants were browner, the ground was muddier, and getting colder only made everyone *even slower*.

Rylie thought she was going to go crazy.

But eventually, the moment did arrive. It was early in the morning on the following day. Abel went off the trail to shoot a few devices he spotted in the trees, and Rylie, Seth, and Bekah jumped at the chance. They left as soon as he was out of sight.

"Abel is going to kill me," Rylie muttered, keeping an eye out for him as they ran deeper into the forest.

"He would have to get to you before the Union does." Bekah's cheeks were colorless, and she didn't even attempt to smile at her weak joke. "I can't believe I'm going back there willingly."

"We'll make it fast," Seth said. "In and out. We have to kill their generators and grab the phone. It will be easy."

"Easy. Yeah. Right." That didn't really comfort Rylie at all.

She remembered the route to the old settlement on the mountain, even though it had been a long time since she was tied up in its church. Bekah was too disoriented to find it, and Seth had difficulty keeping up with them, so Rylie took the lead.

They must have traveled for a couple of hours, but time made no sense in the forest. But the smell of gun oil and silver was easy to follow. When the trees started to thin, she stopped.

"It's about a quarter of a mile that way," she said, pointing. Fear and anxiety clenched her throat shut. It was hard to breathe, much less speak.

"There are black boxes everywhere," Bekah said, staring up at the trees. "They'll know we're coming. Should we shoot them?"

Seth checked his rifle and the extra ammunition he had taken from Abel's duffel bag. "In about two minutes, it won't matter if they know we're coming. You should shift now."

That was the part that worried Rylie the most—the part where she was not only supposed to change on command, but not kill her friends while she did it. But she didn't need to worry about the first one. Going in to fight with the Union had already stirred her wolf, and her fingernails were itching.

Tears burned in the corners of her eyes. "What if I kill someone?"

"I'll be there," Seth said firmly. "You won't."

Bekah gave them a faint smile. "Good luck, guys."

She stripped down and changed. She had the process down to an art; it only took a few moments, and if it hurt, there was no way to tell. Fur swept down her body in elegant lines. Her tail extended with a crunch at the same time as her face. She lowered to all fours before her popping knees made her fall.

Before long, a wolf with a honey-blond coat stood in front of them. It shook blood out of its fur. Even in a nice transition, there was no way to stop some minor injuries.

Rylie was sick with nerves. She grabbed Seth's hand.

"I don't want to do this," she whispered.

He kissed her gently. "Trust me, Rylie. And trust yourself."

Seth backed away, but he never looked away from her. He trusted her. She knew it with every fiber of her being.

Rylie shut her eyes and let go.

•○•

Yasir was getting his unit ready to move out when one of the witches interrupted him.

"You should see this," Raven wheezed, out of breath.

He followed her to the monitoring RV. The outpost was empty aside from his team and a few witches who had stayed behind to keep an eye on the werewolves locked in the church; it was like walking through a ghost town.

"What is it?" he asked, leaning over her chair to punch the button that brought up recent alarms. The list was huge. It registered movements every thirty seconds, which included everything from squirrels and fat caterpillars to herds of deer.

"We've been following the two surviving groups of thirty-twenties since the beach assault," Raven said. "The smaller one is heading up the mountain. I think they're going to the peak."

Yasir nodded impatiently. "Right. I was about to address that with my team."

"The big one is going around to the other side of the forest, maybe to attempt an escape." When he opened his mouth to speak again, she hurriedly went on. "I know the other unit is already going after them with the vehicle fleet. They should converge in thirty minutes."

"Yeah, so we'll have all the wolves confined or killed by the end of the day. What's the problem?"

"If those are the only two groups left... then what's this?"

Raven highlighted a few recent alarms he hadn't noticed. Their corresponding coordinates looked familiar.

He scanned the monitor with the map and saw a single red dot that had broken off from the other, bigger clusters of dots.

It was right outside the camp.

He breathed a swear word in Arabic. Yasir wasn't a fluent speaker, but his grandpa had taught him a few of the worst phrases for fun when he was a kid, and he liked to save them for special occasions. And there was no occasion more special than realizing there was something unfriendly on his front doorstep.

Yasir burst out of the RV. "Team! Move it!" he roared.

His teammates ran over. They were only half-prepared for an attack. Jakob had his ammo belt on, but no gun. Stripes only had knives.

"What is it?" Jakob asked.

"I think Eleanor is back," Yasir said grimly. "We're delaying the mission."

He grabbed ropes off a supply table as they ran out to meet the red dot in the forest.

But it wasn't Eleanor waiting for them.

Seth stood on top of a felled tree with the rifle Yasir had given him. There were two very large, very shaggy wolves standing in front of him—about three times the size of the average timber wolf. One of them was growling, drooling, and trying to chew off its own foot as the other sniffed the air.

Both of them turned golden-eyed stares on the men when they burst through the trees. The moon wasn't for three days, but they were unmistakably, undeniably werewolves, and the unit had nothing more than a knife among them.

"Afternoon," Seth said cheerfully.

The werewolves jumped.

They moved like lightning, too inconceivably fast for his mind to follow. Stripes screamed. A furry body knocked Yasir into a tree hard enough to make the breath rush out of his lungs. He flung his arms over his face with a ragged gasp, bracing himself for the bite—but it never came.

Both wolves darted past them and into the compound. Seth followed.

"Hey!" Yasir shouted, but the boy didn't stop. He dropped to his knees to check on Stripes. "What happened? Where did it get you?"

"My arm! My arm!"

He checked his teammate's arm. There was no sign of a bite, but there was a really big scrape on his elbow.

"Get back on your feet, you idiot!" Yasir barked. "Jakob, with me!"

They scrambled back to camp.

The amount of damage two werewolves could do in ten seconds was incredible. Witches screamed and ran. The wolf with brown fur had a mouthful of wires from the generator and chewed them until the engine sputtered and died.

But it was nothing compared to the gold wolf, which seemed to have gone crazy. It tore through tents, knocked over everything in its path, and snapped at witches. The women weren't prepared for attack. All they could do was flee.

In the middle of it all, Seth ran for the supply tent.

Yasir chased him.

He found the boy digging through the box of confiscated items. "What are you doing?" he demanded, seizing Seth by the shoulder.

"I needed this." He held up a cell phone. "And I needed to keep you guys from killing anyone else. That's what the girls are doing. We'll be out of here in a minute."

"Are you *insane*?"

Seth shrugged. "Sorry."

Yasir was about ready to shoot the boy himself, but before he could decide what to do, the tent posts buckled. The canvas ripped. The gold werewolf stuck its head through the hole, slavering and wild-eyed.

Maybe it was his imagination—werewolves didn't *think*, not like humans did—but Yasir was almost certain that it looked at his hand on Seth's arm and got angrier. It knocked the tent over to lunge for him.

"Whoa!" Seth shouted, jumping in front of Yasir with his hands out. The werewolf stopped dead. "It's okay! You don't want to do that!"

The werewolf twitched. A ripple spread through its fur. But it didn't attack.

Yasir grabbed a shotgun off the rack.

He didn't have time to load it and fire. Seth ran out of the tent, and the wolf followed him like a white-gold blur.

They made a line straight for the forest.

"Bekah!" Seth yelled, and the second wolf stopped mauling the generators to join them. The lights had already gone out in the RV and on all of the tents. The cables were totally destroyed.

The brown wolf ran to him.

At the same moment, Stripes and Jakob appeared. They dropped to their knees in front of their commander with shotguns and aimed.

Everything moved in slow motion for Yasir. He processed the way they were aiming—with Seth in the line of fire—and the bounding motion of the werewolf as it jumped over a tent. Someone was about to get seriously hurt, and he was pretty sure it wouldn't be the werewolves.

"Stop!" Yasir yelled. "Stop!"

Stripes shot him a disbelieving look. "Seriously?"

Jakob got to his feet and took a step forward before Yasir grabbed his shoulder. "Leave them alone."

Seth met Yasir's gaze over the back of the gold werewolf. "Thanks."

They rushed out of the camp. A sick feeling eased its way into Yasir's gut as he watched them leave. "You let them go," Stripes said. "What were you thinking?"

"Seth's not our enemy."

His teammates exchanged looks, and something subtle shifted in the unit's dynamic in that moment.

It reminded Yasir of the time he was on a special mission in Afghanistan. His commander at the time had snapped from the stress of fighting and had started to make bad decisions. Yasir and his brothers ended up taking charge, and the instant they agreed to do it had felt very much like what was happening between Stripes and Jakob.

It was what happened when the men lost faith in the authority. But he wasn't one of the soldiers anymore. He was the commander.

"Check the damage to the generator," Yasir said. Neither of them moved. "You heard me, Stripes. I won't tell you again."

The other man moved, but it was slow. Jakob put a hand to his earpiece and switched channels so that Yasir wouldn't hear his conversation. He walked away muttering to the commander of another unit.

When both of them were gone, he let himself sag against a tree trunk and scrubbed a hand over his face. He usually didn't dare show weakness in front of the men.

"This is bad," he said to the empty, destroyed camp.

Twenty-One

Jealousy

Rylie and Bekah ran without stopping for almost an hour. Seth struggled to keep up with them.

He was afraid that he would have to fight Rylie to get her back to her human form, but when they finally stopped in a clearing well off the beaten path, she was the first to turn back. It only took a few seconds. She collapsed to her knees with a groan.

"Are you okay?" Seth asked, grabbing her hand.

She leaned her head into his shoulder. "I think so. Did I kill anyone?"

"No. You did great."

Bekah shook herself out. "Did they follow us? Are we alive?"

"I think we made it. I don't feel dead, at least," he said. He wrapped his arm around Rylie and helped her to her feet, but she didn't need the support. "Now we just have to find our way back to the group."

"That won't be a problem," Bekah said, pointing.

Seth looked up to see his brother rush through the forest to them, nose to the wind and a gun in his hand.

"What is wrong with you?" Abel hissed, searching Rylie and Bekah with his eyes. Finding them both alive and unhurt didn't seem to mollify him in the slightest.

"What's wrong with me?" Seth laughed. "Come on, man. I have Stephanie's phone, and the Union won't be able to use their equipment to find us now. We destroyed their generator. Mission successful."

"You left without telling me!"

"You wouldn't have let us go if you knew what we had planned. What else was I supposed to do?"

"Not run off on a stupid suicide mission! That's what!"

"Don't you think we should keep moving?" Rylie asked. "We're not *that* far from the Union camp, and it's kind of cold."

The guys fell into a tense, uncomfortable silence, and it followed them all the way up the mountain.

They didn't catch up until nightfall. The wolves had camped a mile away from the peak of Gray Mountain. There weren't many trees to shield them at that elevation, and the wind was harsh and biting.

Stephanie hurried over to meet them. "Did you get it?" she asked Seth, and he gave her the cell phone.

Abel rolled his eyes. "Of course. This was *your* idea."

They ignored him.

Stephanie turned on her cell phone. As soon as the screen loaded, she turned it off again. "No reception. I suppose that's not a surprise. I'm sure I could get a signal on the highway."

"I'll take you," Seth said. "Now that the hunters don't have sensors, two people should slip past them with no problem."

Abel puffed up his chest. "I'll go, too."

"Very well. We should leave immediately."

Stephanie gathered her things. When Rylie moved to get up, too, Abel loomed over her. "Stay here and watch your kittens," he said. He jerked his chin toward Bekah. "Especially that one."

Rylie rolled her eyes. "I didn't find Bekah in a dumpster."

"You get the idea."

"Don't listen to him. You can come if you want," Seth said.

"No, it's fine with me," Rylie said. She was pale and trembling. "I don't mind keeping an eye on everything here. Just come back as fast as you can."

Seth kissed her goodbye, and then he left with Abel and Stephanie.

The trip down the mountain took the better part of the day, even using the main trails. Traveling with a human doctor was completely different than traveling with two werewolves. Stephanie had to take frequent breaks, and she refused to let Abel carry her.

She turned her phone on periodically to see if she could find reception, but she didn't get a single bar until they had passed the girls' camp and had the highway in sight again. They didn't run into a single hunter on the way—or any other werewolves, for that matter. The forest was eerily silent.

"Where is everyone? You couldn't go a half mile without tripping on another werewolf a couple of days ago," Abel asked as Stephanie held the phone over her head in search of the best reception.

"We haven't seen anyone new in a couple of days," she said. "I think our group is all that remains. It will make the Union's job much easier to wipe everyone out when the full moon rises tomorrow night."

Seth gazed up at the mountain, wishing he could see where Rylie was camped at that moment. There were only about twenty wolves up there, although he hadn't gotten a good count lately, and he didn't know any names.

Were those all the werewolves left in the entire world?

He suddenly felt sad, but he wasn't sure why. Seth had spent his entire life trying to destroy the werewolf population. But being on the verge of success wasn't satisfying at all. After seeing his brother and his girlfriend go through the change, he wouldn't wish it on anyone, but it didn't seem fair to let them die out, either.

Abel and Seth hung back to watch for attacks while Stephanie stood in the road to call.

Her conversation with Scott didn't last long. When she returned to them, her face was grim. "Levi's heading up the mountain to be with Bekah. He already left. But Scott said he can't get the van to us; they've destroyed part of the highway."

"It doesn't matter," Abel said. "Scott's van wouldn't fit everyone. It's only got ten seats. We could barely cram a dozen really friendly people in there." He rolled his eyes. "And I know Rylie wouldn't leave without everyone else."

"It seems that the wolves are trapped." The doctor looked grim. "Well, I told Scott I would meet him down the road. It's not safe for me to be with the pack anymore—I'm not interested in growing that much facial hair. If either of you would like to escape, this would be the time to do it."

The brothers exchanged looks.

"Thanks, but we've got to finish this," Seth said.

Stephanie looked at them like she thought they were both crazy, but she shook Seth's hand when she gave him the cell phone. "Good luck. Scott and I will see what we can do about getting another van. If you make it until tomorrow morning—and if the hunters don't have you—then call me. We'll rendezvous with the survivors and return to the sanctuary."

With that cheerful sentiment, she headed down the road. Abel pulled a face at her back. "Jeez. I can barely handle all the optimism."

They headed back up the mountain without talking. Abel completely ignored him. Seth had thought a lot about getting to see his brother again, but despite imagining their reunion a dozen different ways, he hadn't expected such overt unfriendliness.

He didn't want to be the first to talk, but when they finally drew close to Camp Silver Brook, he got sick of the quiet.

"Okay. What's the problem, man?" Seth asked.

Abel gave him a flat look and didn't speak.

"Do you still think I'm with the hunters, even after what we did at the outpost? Is that why you've been such a jerk to me for the last few hours?" he asked. After a moment, Abel shook his head stiffly. "Then what's eating you?"

His eyes were shadowed with thought. It took him a full minute to respond. "How's this? If you hurt Rylie, I'll break your head."

Seth's eyes went wide. He couldn't help it. His shock was shortly followed by a creeping suspicion, which he tried to suppress with a laugh. "Okay. What have you done with my brother?"

But his brother didn't laugh back. "I mean it."

Seth crossed his arms and stared down Abel. The older brother was a lot taller, a lot broader, and a lot stronger. And he had straightened his spine to show off every inch of that advantage he had. He was actually trying to be intimidating.

Seth felt a little bit like he was going crazy. The last time he saw Abel, he had still been in denial about being a werewolf, and he blamed Rylie for what happened. A lot had apparently changed in the months since then.

"What are you getting at?" Seth asked.

"I know what you two did, and I'm saying, I'll break your head if you hurt her," Abel said.

"That's not your business, man."

"Like hell. She's my pack."

"Your pack? Do you know what that sounds like?"

"It sounds like I'm a werewolf, that's what. And you know what else? I *am* a werewolf. We both are, me and Rylie." He thumped his fist on his chest. "There's no cure for this. It's a life sentence. But we've been getting by okay on our own, getting through this together. What have you been doing? Going to school? Studying for college? Rylie could have used you these last few months." His jaw tightened. "I could have used you."

"Gwyn needed me," Seth said.

"More than your brother and your girlfriend?"

"Well, yeah. Neither of you are dying." He stepped up, invading Abel's space. "But this isn't about that, is it? You're jealous."

Abel barked a laugh. "Jealous?"

"I'm not stupid, bro."

"And I don't know what you're getting at. *Bro.*"

"You've got a thing for Rylie now. That's what I'm getting at," Seth said.

He guessed Abel's motion a heartbeat before he made it— the way his arms flexed, the shift in his weight. Seth ducked, and the punch swung harmlessly over his head. He drove his shoulder into Abel's gut and knocked them both into a tree.

A rock caught his foot. He lost his balance and tumbled, dragging Abel down with him.

They slid a few feet down the hill, swinging useless kicks and punches at each other that couldn't seem to land.

The brothers splashed into a shallow part of the brook. Seth rose up and socked Abel squarely in the jaw. He had always been good at taking a hit, and he was even better since becoming a werewolf. It didn't even faze him.

Abel kicked Seth's feet out from under him. Seth fell, and his head cracked on a rock.

"Ouch! Hey, that hurt!" Seth sat up and touched the back of his neck. A little blood came away on his fingers.

"You sissy. That wasn't even a big rock."

Abel didn't try to attack him again. He pulled Seth to his feet. They stood on separate parts of the bank to inspect their various scrapes in silence, which was a lot more comfortable than it had been before the fight.

Once Seth decided he wasn't concussed, he looked up at his brother, who had already healed completely. "Feel better now?"

"No. I'm going to steal your girl." Abel made an evil demon face with his eyes crossed and his tongue sticking out. Seth snorted.

"You're so full of it."

"I told you I would break your head, didn't I?"

Seth shoved him. Abel shoved him back. It wasn't serious anymore. "Come on. Tell me what's wrong. I won't pick on you for being a big wimp and sharing your feelings. Scout's honor."

Abel muttered a curse. "You know Rylie's been thinking about killing herself?"

"She mentioned it."

"So you get here, and it's all better? She's all smiles and sunshine again? You get to ride in with other hunters—with *Mom*—after being away for months, but you've still got the magical hero touch. And then you don't listen to me. You argue with me, and *disrespect* me. But it's all fine, because you're the hero. I don't get it. It's bull."

"Seriously?"

He rubbed a hand over the back of his neck. "I was worried about you guys."

"Sorry," Seth said.

"So... yeah." Abel threw a punch into Seth's arm that didn't hurt. "Me and Rylie are just pack. You know I wouldn't do that to you anyway."

"Yep. I know."

"Great. Now come here, you stupid kid," he said, holding out an arm.

It was a short hug. Seth slammed his hand on Abel's back, and his brother did the same for him. And then they took big steps back and didn't look at each other.

"You're still ugly as sin," Seth said. "And your goatee is stupid."

"And you're still scrawny."

Which was pretty much brother speak for, "I missed you." That was the best Seth thought he would ever get out of him. "Thanks for looking out for Rylie."

Abel snorted. "Whatever." They trudged up the hill they had just fallen down, trying to shake themselves dry. Seth's boots made a wet squelching noise with every step. "I'll still break your head if you hurt Rylie."

"And what if *I* do the hurting?"

The voice came from above.

They looked up at the same time, but it wasn't fast enough. A dark shape dropped from the branches.

Eleanor landed on Abel, bringing her connected fists down on his skull with a *crack*. Even for a werewolf, the impact was too much. His eyes blanked immediately. He slumped, unconscious.

Seth moved to draw his gun, but her pistol was already in her hand.

"Forget about it," she said, aiming it steadily toward his forehead. She drew a silver-bladed knife from her belt and pressed it to Abel's throat. "Throw your gun down or I'll end his life right now."

"You would kill your son?"

She didn't even falter. "I don't have a werewolf son."

Seth dropped his gun. She picked it up and put it over her shoulder, then gestured. He realized that her thigh was bandaged. His shot the other night had hit its target, but it didn't seem to have stopped her.

"Link your hands behind your head and turn around. Walk that way. You're coming with me," she said.

Pulse jackhammering in his throat, he did as she ordered.

He heard a wet *crunch* as soon as he turned around. Seth spun.

Eleanor had driven the knife into Abel's stomach. He was unconscious and didn't react.

Rage and instinct took over all at once, overpowering his sense of self-preservation. With a roar, Seth threw himself at Eleanor.

She fired a gunshot. He felt it buzz past his ear.

He froze.

"I think I told you to turn around and walk," she said, her face twisted with righteous wrath. Seth looked over her shoulder at his brother, bleeding from a silver-inflicted wound on his stomach, and thought of all those bodies that the Union had found.

"How could you?" he whispered. "That's *Abel*."

"Walk."

Leaving his brother was physically painful, but he couldn't finish off Eleanor if she killed him, too. He began to march. "Where are we going?"

"We're going back to the Union compound. Yasir's not in charge anymore, which leaves an army at my disposal. And we're marching tomorrow night." He could practically hear her evil grin. "It's almost full moon, after all."

Twenty-Two

Destiny

Seth kept his hands behind his head as Eleanor marched him back to the Union outpost. He considered making a break for it. He had to get back to Abel. He had to see if he was okay, had to get him to Stephanie so she could patch up his wound...

But Eleanor seemed to know what he was thinking. She dug the pistol into his neck.

He gritted his teeth and kept moving.

Even though he knew he couldn't talk his mom out of anything—not her choice of breakfast cereal, much less her choice of tactics—he had to try. "We don't have to do this."

"Shut up."

She kept up a grueling pace. Every time he slowed, she jabbed the gun into the back of his skull again to prod him forward. And she didn't give him any opportunity to fight back. Seth wasn't sure he could have won against her anyway.

When they walked for over two hours without a break, he decided to try talking again. "Why did you run away from the Union?"

He thought that would earn him another hard poke, but Eleanor said, "Yasir was out to kill me. I had to move."

"They found the werewolves you've been killing. Three of them."

"That's only the start," she said. "There are another dozen they haven't found."

"As humans, Mom? I thought we always agreed to wait until the moons to hunt. It's what Dad wanted."

"They would be too much to handle if we didn't thin the herd before the moon. Once the Alpha's picked, it's going to get bad."

Seth blinked. "Alpha?"

She finally stopped marching. She took a roll of paper from one of her cargo pants pockets, flattened it out, and shoved the pages in his face. There were holes along the sides where it had been fed through a really old printer. After being carried around for years, they were yellowed and tissue-thin.

"Look at this. Look!"

Seth took them from her just to get them out of his face. He recognized the handwriting scrawled in red ink along the margins. It belonged to his dad.

"Is this from when he wrote that stupid book?"

She ripped it from his hands. He raised a fist, and she responded by raising the gun. "Show respect." Eleanor shook the pages at him. "Here's what nobody knows, boy: this is all part of a bigger plan. The plan of something *evil*. Those werewolves weren't the only ones summoned here. We were, too. The hunters and the witches and the heroes. It's destiny."

"You've lost me."

"Look," she said again, jamming the gun in her belt and shuffling through the pages to the end. "Your daddy wrote about it. I found this only a month ago."

Seth skimmed the page as she held it up to his face. It was a solid block of rambling, stream-of-consciousness text. The book he published had been practical, like a cookbook for killing werewolves, and didn't have any spiritual nonsense. But the words "animal spirits" and "gods" were all over the place in this text. His dad must have been drunk when he wrote it.

"The chapter says this isn't the first time werewolves have almost gone extinct. Their gods have a plan for handling it. They call the werewolves back to the mountain, and the gods choose the strongest of them to become Alpha. It's all going down tomorrow night. The Alpha's, uh..." She checked the page. "The Alpha's *coronation* is a bloodbath where the hunters all die. And those *things* have always won. But we can turn it around this time!"

"Or we could leave peacefully," Seth suggested.

Her fist tightened on the page. "Werewolves might be monsters, but at least they got one thing right." Eleanor shoved her face into his. It took all of Seth's willpower not to back away. "They kill the runts of the litter."

Death threats from his mom used to hurt his feelings. Not anymore. Instead, he missed Aunt Gwyn, and the smell of baking pies, and getting called "Einstein" like it was a good thing. "Love you too, Mom," he said dully.

Her face softened. "I love you, baby, but these werewolves have put you under a spell. You're sick. Once they're all dead, you'll be better. We'll be a family again. I meant it when I said I wanted that."

"Do you see Abel in that family?" Seth asked.

Eleanor patted his back. She didn't have to respond. He knew the answer.

They went back to walking.

Jakob greeted them at the perimeter of the Union outpost. The other kopis didn't look surprised to see them. "Took you long enough," he said, escorting them into the camp.

"You knew we were coming?" Seth asked.

The older man didn't respond. He did, however, steady his gun on Seth. Apparently he hadn't forgotten about the attack yet.

The Union was getting ready to mobilize. The generator was still a mess, so they didn't have power in their tents, but they had hooked up a couple of the SUVs to power a few lights. The monitors were all dark, though, and he didn't see anything connected to the motion sensors anymore. As long as the werewolves kept moving, they would be safe.

Eleanor sat Seth in a chair by the gun rack and roped his arms to his sides. It was too familiar a position. At least he wasn't under a mobile home again.

"Good to see you, kid," groaned a voice.

Seth twisted around. Yasir was tied on the ground behind the table with a bruise-blackened face.

"What happened to you?"

"Mutiny." He worked his mouth around and spit blood onto a patch of grass. "Eleanor stole one of our satellite phones and contacted command. She said I had gone rogue. They ordered the team to disable me and put her in charge."

Seth groaned. "Sounds like Eleanor."

"Gotta say, kid, I kind of hate your mom."

He watched as his mother helped the Union prepare. Her eyes were alight with fire. Standing at the head of an army was Eleanor in her natural element, and she looked like she was having fun, even though she had just stabbed her son and left him for dead in the forest.

"Yeah," Seth said. "Me too."

•○•

Rylie paced back and forth across the trail, gnawing on her thumbnail.

Seth, Abel, and Stephanie had been gone for an entire day and night, and there was no sign of them. Rylie hadn't been too worried for the first few hours, but when the day wore on and they didn't return, she started to feel a sense of unease. And when clouds consumed the sun and it started drizzling, she *really* started to worry.

The werewolves moved around to find shelter under the patchy trees, but Rylie kept pacing. After working on a ranch in the snow, a little rain was nothing.

"Hey," Bekah said, joining her at the head of the trail. She used a woolen blanket to shield her head from the weather. "Any sign of them?"

"Not yet."

The other girl inched over to share her blanket with Rylie. "It's probably okay. That's a really big forest out there, and I think it changes shape every time we go through it. You know? Like when the mountain wants us to get somewhere, it only takes an hour to walk across the whole thing. But sometimes it takes days."

"The mountain's not alive, and it can't warp the forest. So don't talk like that. It's creepy." Rylie held up one corner of the sheet, but without the ability to release her nervous energy with pacing, she ended up tapping her foot and fidgeting instead. "The moon's going to rise in a couple of hours."

"I'm sure they'll be back before that."

Rylie cast a sideways look at Bekah. "But what if they're dead or something?"

"I don't think there's any reason to jump to that conclusion."

"There are a bunch of men out there with guns, so I think there's lots of good reason to worry about it."

"Maybe a little," Bekah conceded. "But if I trusted anyone to survive on a mountain with armed hunters, it would be Seth and Abel. They *are* hunters. They can take care of themselves."

She was probably right. It still didn't do anything to alleviate Rylie's fears.

But then something moved at the bottom of the dark trail, and she perked up. The rain suppressed her sense of smell, so she couldn't tell if it was friend or foe, but she didn't think an enemy would walk up to them quite so obviously.

Bekah recognized him first. She dropped the blanket with a shriek. "Levi!"

She raced down the trail and flew into her brother's arms. Rylie followed a little slower, trying to manage a smile. She was happy to see him. Really. And Levi looked like he'd had a rough couple of weeks—he was muddy and exhausted. But even though she knew it was horrible, she would have much preferred it to be Seth or Abel.

"Scott and I got here yesterday. He couldn't drive this far— the road's blocked—but I ran as fast as I could," he said, setting his sister down. His brown curls were plastered to his forehead. He had managed to bring shorts with him somehow, but no shirt or shoes. Bekah and Levi were both pretty good at keeping their clothes when they shifted. "Are you okay?"

Bekah's chin trembled. It took her a moment to work up her usual glowing smile. "It's been pretty bad. But we'll be okay."

"Did you see anyone on the way up?" Rylie asked.

"Like who? You mean the men in black? I saw a few, but I didn't go near them."

Her stomach pitched. "Let's talk about this somewhere drier."

Rylie led him to camp. Toshiko had built a small campfire between two rocks with a blanket to shelter it. She smiled at the sight of them, but had long since given up trying to communicate. She left as soon as they approached.

They settled around the fire, warming their hands and trying to dry their clothes while Bekah filled Levi in on everything that happened.

"You attacked a bunch of hunters?" he asked.

She gave another weak smile. "And I ate a generator."

He laughed. It struck Rylie as a weird sound. They hadn't been laughing a lot since they had reached the forest. "That's kind of awesome. No wonder they looked so mad."

"Where did you see them?"

"They've got a camp down there." He waved at the trees. "I didn't take a lot of time to look around. It looks like they're going to march soon."

A twig snapped nearby, cutting him off.

Rylie spun to face it with a growl, but it wasn't an attack by hunters. A lone figure staggered out of the trees to the south, and he was hunched over like something was hurting him.

Abel.

He groaned and fell to his knees. Rylie managed to beat Bekah to his side.

"Oh my God! Are you okay? What happened?"

Abel held out the hand he had been pressing to his side. His fingers were black with blood. "Mom stabbed me," he said. His eyes had a hard time focusing. It was like he looked over Rylie's shoulder instead of at her face. "Silver knife."

She dragged him to the fire and helped him stretch out. She was strong, but she still needed Levi's help to shift him. Abel glared at Levi.

"Hey, you found us. I haven't missed your ugly face," Abel said.

"Well, being a jerk is probably a good sign, but I don't think *that* is," Levi said, lifting Abel's shirt to see the wound. "Where's Stephanie?"

"She's with Scott," Abel groaned.

That didn't seem like the more important question. "Where's Seth?" Rylie asked, grabbing Abel's hand. His bloody fingers slipped in her grip.

That got his attention. He finally looked at her. Really looked at her.

"Eleanor," he said.

Rylie felt like she was going to fall over. It was the worst thing she could have possibly imagined. She would prefer Seth to defect to the Union than end up in his mom's grasp.

"I should check to see if there's silver in there," Levi announced at about the same time he started digging around in the wound with his fingers.

Abel's eyes clenched shut, and his teeth ground together. Rylie held his hand tighter. "How could she do this to you?" she asked, her voice thick with tears.

"Kind of like… this." He made a weak stabbing motion in the air.

Rylie laughed wetly. "I got that part."

Abel didn't have the energy to joke for much longer. Levi removed his hand. "If there's anything in there, I can't find it. Stephanie picked a good time to leave."

"He'll heal when the moon rises," Bekah said. "Right?"

Not if there was silver in the wound. If Eleanor stabbed him, that didn't seem too likely. But Rylie remembered how much those injuries burned. He wasn't going to have a fun time healing, either way.

It wasn't a good answer, so Rylie kept it to herself.

"The Union is moving and Eleanor's hunting," she said. "This is really bad. We have to go. We can't be here when they come looking."

"It's getting way too late for that," Bekah said. "It's not long until moonrise."

Levi used bottled water to rinse his hands off. "They'll come to this peak, right? We can hide nearby until everyone changes, and then when they move in, we attack."

Nobody had a better plan to suggest. The cloud cover made it darker than it should have been at that hour, but night wasn't far away.

"Come on, Levi," Bekah said. "Let's talk to everyone else."

They went to rouse the other wolves, but Rylie stayed with Abel. He hadn't let go of her hand. "You have to save Seth," he said.

"How?"

"Go looking. Find him. Help him."

Rylie had been thinking the same thing, but she never would have expected Abel to tell her to put herself in danger. He was the one who didn't want her collecting "dumpster kittens," much less tracking down his mother. And Rylie wasn't exactly the heroic type. She was the "go crazy and eat farmers" type.

She bit her lip. "I don't know if I can take Eleanor."

"You have to," Abel said. He tried to sit up, then flinched and lay back. "Oh, man. You can beat her as a wolf. You're fast. You're strong."

"What if I can't shift before moonrise?" She had changed outside the Union camp, but she had Seth to help her. She didn't think she could do it alone.

"So what?" He grimaced and lifted his head to look at the wound. "I'll try to come find you as soon as I shift and heal. But she's got a head start. You have to find him, you have to change, and you have to save him. Promise."

She stared out at all the werewolves as they gathered around at Bekah and Levi. They were talking loudly, explaining what little plans they had, and everyone listened attentively. Bekah would do a good job rallying them. She was nice, and she was strong, and everyone admired her.

Rylie wasn't nice. She wasn't strong. She was so horribly weak—so helpless when it came to the wolf.

But Seth needed her.

She nodded. "I'll do it." It was simultaneously the easiest and the hardest promise she had ever made.

He relaxed, like all the pain had suddenly vanished from his wound. His eyelids drooped. "Good," Abel said. He gave her a faint half-smile that looked a lot like Seth's. "Thanks." His fingers fell from hers. She watched his chest for a moment to make sure he kept breathing, but he had only passed out from the pain.

Glancing around to make sure nobody was watching, she slipped away from the group into darkness.

•○•

Rylie waited to change until she put distance between herself and the dim glow of their camp. Her wolf didn't want to leave the peak of Gray Mountain, but she was done negotiating with her beast. She was the one in charge.

"You hear me?" she whispered to herself when she reached a cliff overlooking the river. It was a silver snake of moonlight running through the black forest. Falling rain dappled its surface. "I'm in charge. And I say we change."

The wolf remained silent.

Rylie looked at her hands, imagining the claws that she had seen grow from the tips far too often. She remembered the itch of fur sprouting from her skin, and the ache of her jaw elongating.

Seth needs me.

Love was pretty good motivation to do the impossible.

She began to shift.

It hurt. It always hurt, and there was no way around it. But when she didn't fight the change so hard, it was easier to ride it out.

She sank to her knees and watched her feet turn into paws. The toes shortened as the foot lengthened. It traveled up her calf and inverted her knee with a slick crunch that felt like getting struck by a baseball bat, and a cry escaped her lips. It came out as more of a yelp. Her outsides were changing slower than her insides, which felt like a mass of twisting worms. She already had a wolf's vocal cords.

Rylie focused on the pale patch of silvery moon she could see through the clouds as her face cracked and shifted. Tears leaped to her eyes. She let the teeth fall from her mouth, and the hair from her scalp, and let the wolf deal with the pain.

Its mind emerged like a vast shadow settling over Rylie's thoughts. It didn't blot her mind out, but it weighed her down. It was so happy to be in the forest, rain and all.

A few minutes later, they were complete, and a wolf stood where a girl had before.

She lifted her nose to the breeze. Picking out smells when it was wet was difficult, but not impossible. The wolf was especially attuned to the odor of silver, and she could smell it farther down the mountain.

Rylie and the wolf ran. She darted across the mountain, leaping nimbly through the forest like golden lightning.

Once she had the smell, it was easy to locate Eleanor. Rylie was surprised to find her with all the other hunters. Levi was right. The Union was marching, and they were making a direct line for the peak of Gray Mountain to make a stand. They took up the entire trail and didn't seem worried about being spotted. Why should they? There were tons of men with guns. They didn't have to be afraid of anything.

Rylie swung wide, making a loop around the long line of people. She climbed onto a ridge overlooking them and smelled the wind again. The sprinkling rain was dying down.

A dozen armed men. A half-dozen unarmed women. And one woman in the lead, dragging two men in ropes.

Two men?

She bounced down the rocks to get a closer look, careful to stay within the trees where they wouldn't see her.

Rylie recognized Seth, whose wrists were tethered to a long rope held by his mother, but she didn't know who the other man was. He was even more beaten than Seth. His skin was earthen brown, his hair had a militaristic cut, and he wore the same black uniform as everyone else. His face resonated with the wolf. She must have seen him at the Union camp and didn't remember him, even if her beast did.

The wolf wanted to dive in, but her human mind held her back. There were too many people. Too many guns. Too much silver. She needed to wait until the right moment.

She would follow them. She would wait.

And as soon as she got a chance, she would kill Eleanor.

Twenty-Three

Alpha

The hunters reached the peak of Gray Mountain at nightfall.

"Eighteen minutes to moonrise," Jakob said. They all had watches with countdown timers.

Eleanor stalked across the rocks, narrowed eyes scanning the mountaintop. Seth stumbled after her. His shoulder bumped into Yasir. She had given them a short line between their arms, and she seemed to enjoy dragging them around like dogs.

"There's nobody here," Stripes said.

Seth stopped behind his mother. They stood on a raised stone platform slicked by ice. The rain hadn't melted any of it.

It wasn't Seth's first time on top of Gray Mountain. It wasn't even the first time he had been dragged there against his will. Nothing had changed since the year before, either, but he had to stare at it. The rocks were too incredible not to stare.

At first glance, the rock formation on top of the mountain looked like it had been placed deliberately. There was no way erosion would have left pillars standing naturally in a neat spiral. Each successive rock was bigger than the last, creating stairs to a single point that towered over everything else.

But Seth had taken some pretty close looks at the rocks, and there was no indication they had been laid out by humans.

He hadn't seen any tool marks, or other signs of how someone had dragged such massive boulders to the tallest place in the entire forest. He used to think that it had to be natural. But he didn't think the fact that it looked like a temple was coincidental anymore.

"What is this place?" Yasir asked, breath fogging from his lips.

"It's a holy place." Seth's voice echoed strangely in the night. All of the other hunters had fallen silent as they stared around at the deep shadows, hands gripping their guns so tightly that they shook.

Eleanor glared at the cloudy sky. On top of the temple of the animal spirits, she looked like a force of wild magic herself. Her eyes burned with challenge. Her arms were spread wide to the moist wind with her feet braced on the rocks, like a challenge to the gods to smite her where she stood.

Nothing attacked her. She dropped her hands and faced Seth.

"You call it holy," she said. "I say it's unholy. Pagan. This is where a bloody coronation happens tonight. This is where the Alpha is chosen."

Yasir gave a harsh laugh. "There's nothing spiritual about any of this. You know what werewolves are? A disease."

Very casually, Eleanor backhanded him. Her knuckles cracked against his jaw. Seth flinched. He had been on the receiving end of her strikes before. For a human, she had a heck of an arm.

Yasir spit blood onto the ice and glared at Eleanor. She had split his lip. "I swore to protect humans—all humans—when I joined the Union," he said. "But if you hit me again, I will kill you in front of your son and your animal gods and all of these men."

"I'd like to see that," she said with a cruel smile.

"Nine minutes to moonrise," Jakob reported.

The teenage hunter stepped up. He looked more nervous than the rest of them combined. His knees were practically knocking together. "What should we do?"

"Spread out," Eleanor said. "They'll be here soon."

"There are almost twenty werewolves out there," Seth said. "We've got less than twenty men here. I don't think you realize how bad those odds are."

"We don't need to kill twenty wolves. Just the Alpha. Cut off the head…" She sliced her finger across her throat. "Tell me, son. Who do you think is Alpha? The most powerful werewolf is the deadliest. The one who bites the most, but leaves them alive."

It was obvious the direction in which she was taking her narrative. Seth twisted his wrists in his bonds. The knots were too tight, and dug into the soft, fleshy part of his wrist. "Rylie hasn't made other werewolves. She's not the Alpha."

"When she dies, it's all over. And there's no way she'll stay away as long as I have you." Eleanor gave his ropes a hard jerk. He fell to his knees and almost dragged Yasir with him.

"So that's why you got me? This has nothing to do with family, does it?"

"Nothing. And everything." Her eyes were wild. Seth wondered if the Union would have given her command if they had seen it.

"This is going to be a bloodbath," Yasir said. His voice had risen to a shout. "You can't just wait here for them. You have to have a plan, you have to lead—"

Eleanor slapped him again.

With a roar, the commander snapped his ropes. He almost wrenched Seth's arms out of their sockets.

Yasir tackled Eleanor.

She dropped Seth's rope to draw her gun, and he took the opportunity to twist his wrists free. The teenage hunter was only a few feet away. Seth kicked him and wrenched the shotgun out of his hands, spinning to aim it at the boy when the other men tried to move forward.

"Freeze!" he shouted.

Everyone stopped except for Eleanor and Yasir. They rolled across the rocky top of the mountain, wrestling over her pistol.

Jakob took a step.

"Don't move," Seth said, pushing his shotgun into the boy's chest. What was his name? He hadn't bothered to learn it. "I'll do it."

"He won't do it," Jakob told the other men.

He pumped the shotgun and fired into the air.

A wolf's howl responded.

The wail broke the night and sent shivers down Seth's spine. Eleanor and Yasir paused mid-wrestle. She kneeled over her opponent with her fist raised, but she didn't land the punch.

The one howl turned to two, and then three. It was an unearthly sound, like the screaming of ghosts or wailing babies or the bitter cry of the wind through trees.

And then pale shapes emerged below them.

Most of them were still human, but they twisted and writhed as the call of the moon fell upon them. Seth recognized some of the werewolves that had been with Rylie and Abel. A couple had already changed and stalked up the mountain on all fours.

For a moment, the hunters were too transfixed by the shifting bodies to shoot.

Jakob was the first to pull the trigger.

His shot went wide and struck a tree.

It was enough to trigger an attack. The wolves that had already shifted charged up the mountain and crashed into the hunters like two fronts of a storm. Shots fired, growls and howls echoed off the rocks, and Seth didn't wait to see what would happen.

He broke into a run, but stopped at the trees when he recognized one of the people approaching.

Abel's skin was ashen gray, but he was standing—barely. His arm was slung over Levi's shoulder. His stab wound had been bandaged and blood seeped through the gauze. The younger man propped him against a tree, stripped off his shirt, and shifted in a flurry of fur.

Seth had never been so happy to see his brother's ugly face.

"Where's Rylie?" Seth called.

Worry flashed through Abel's eyes. "I thought she was with you. She left to find—*ugh*." He groaned and doubled over.

When he looked up again, his face was growing into a wolf's snout.

Seth backed away slowly. He couldn't shoot Abel if he attacked. He had to run.

But when he turned, Eleanor was behind him. She grabbed his arm, and her fingernails bit into the muscle. She wasn't armed anymore. A quick glance around showed that Yasir had her gun, and was stuck in a standoff with Jakob amidst a roiling mass of bodies.

Seth didn't shoot fast enough. Eleanor ripped the shotgun from his hands.

"Where's your girlfriend?"

"I don't know," he said honestly. *Hopefully very, very far away.*

Eleanor dragged him to the top of the stone pillars. She shook him hard. "Rylie! Come and get him!" she shouted into the night. Her voice was loud enough to carry over the growls and screams.

He didn't know if he believed the werewolves had gods watching over them or not, but he shut his eyes and prayed to them all the same. *Please don't let her come...*

His mother's triumphant cry made his eyes fly open.

A golden wolf erupted from the trees and landed on the rocks below them. Rylie wasn't as big as some of the other werewolves, but she was faster, and she practically flew through the air. Her eyes were bright and clear. There was no hint of silver frenzy left in her.

"No," Seth groaned.

Eleanor dropped him and raised the shotgun.

Rylie darted forward. Her mouth snapped closed on Eleanor's leg. The material of her pants was thick enough that the teeth didn't pierce, but she jerked Seth's mom off her feet.

A massive brown wolf climbed the rocks. He was the color of the stones around him, with flecks of silver in his fur. Seth had only seen his brother in wolf form once, but he recognized Abel instantly.

He went straight for Eleanor and tackled her. Abel tried to bite her. She shoved her arm deep in his mouth so his jaws couldn't close.

Eleanor shoved him off of her, and Seth saw cold calculation flit through her eyes—two werewolves, one gun, not enough bullets—for a half second before she jumped.

She didn't go for Rylie or Abel. She grabbed Seth and smashed the shotgun into his gut.

Both wolves froze. Their golden gazes were unsettlingly calm.

The fight raged on below them, even as everything on top of the pillar went completely still with tension. Seth couldn't tell who was winning anymore. There were bodies scattered across the ground—some wolf, some human. He had a hard time focusing enough to count when there was a gun in his stomach. He flushed with heat.

"Get down, Abel," Eleanor ordered.

It looked like it pained the big wolf to obey her. He slowly backed off the rocks. The parting clouds let silvery moonlight spill across the top of the mountain, like the moon itself wanted to see what was happening.

Then his mother nodded to Rylie.

"Change back."

It was a ridiculous order. She couldn't do that. Nobody could—not even Bekah and Levi. As soon as the moon rose, werewolves were stuck until sunrise.

Rylie's luminous gold eyes met Seth's. He saw the possibilities in them. More than that, he saw the humanity.

She was in control.

"Don't," he whispered.

A shudder ran through her body.

The change back was slow, and almost beautiful. Fingers emerged from paws. A girl's face formed beneath the frightening veneer of the wolf's. She straightened as her fur fell away, and stood straight-backed and proud in front of Eleanor.

One by one, the hunters and werewolves struggling stopped moving to stare, as if Rylie had thrown her arms over her head and started screaming. Yet there was gravity to her silence. A werewolf, human on the full moon—impossible. But she had done it for Seth.

"You see?" the older woman panted, jamming her gun harder into Seth's side. "I told you she's the Alpha!"

"Just let him go," Rylie said.

"Walk to the top. Do it. Go on! Call your gods down, and tell them to save you!"

She turned to obey. Seth watched her retreating back with dismay. There was no way it could end well—there would be no gods waiting to intervene. Eleanor would shoot her, or she would shoot him, but someone was going to die.

The clouds parted as she Rylie to the top of the peak, her bare feet melting the ice as she passed. The moisture on her skin steamed.

A swollen silver moon loomed overhead. It was so huge that it looked like Rylie could reach out with her fingers and brush its surface. Stars scattered in the black patches of the sky, peeking through even the tiniest gap in the clouds. It was like they were watching to see what would happen.

"Call them!" Eleanor shouted.

The fighting stilled as Rylie lifted her arms to the moon, opening her body to its rays. Her eyes fell closed.

Seth broke free of his mother, scrambling up the rocks. "Rylie! Don't do it!"

A flash of pain erupted in his skull. He landed face-first on the stone, and his vision swam. It wasn't until he rolled over and saw his mother holding a rifle with his blood on the metal that he realized she had rammed it into the back of his head.

It was all he could do to roll over and watch as Rylie moved to the very edge of the rocks. She smiled down at him. Her eyes weren't gold anymore. They were filled with the silver of the moon.

"Sorry, Seth," she whispered.

And then she jumped. Her body vanished over the side.

Silence filled the air.

The surviving hunters exchanged looks. The werewolves seemed rooted to where they stood.

"What happened?" Yasir asked. It looked like he had won his fight against Jakob. The other hunter was unconscious at his feet. "Where did she go?"

Eleanor walked carefully up to the highest pillar on the peak. As soon as she left Seth's side, the shaggy brown wolf that was Abel joined him again, standing protectively over his body. He smelled even worse as an animal than as a human, and that was saying a lot.

She glanced at the moon before looking down to search for Rylie.

"Well?" Stripes asked.

"I don't believe it," Eleanor said.

A pale hand shot over the side of the ledge, caught Eleanor's ankle, and jerked her over the side.

Seth's mother screamed as she fell.

The sound cut off with a *crunch*.

Seth felt sick and dizzy and horrified and relieved all at once. Emotion swamped him. He reached up to grab a fistful of Abel's fur to steady himself, and he thought there might have been pain in his brother's reflective eyes.

Slowly, Rylie pulled herself on top of the rocks, and stood on trembling legs—human legs—to look at everyone else. With the moon at her back, her white-gold hair looked like it was aflame with moonlight. Her eyes were still silver, and they were filled with new knowledge. Whatever happened when she faced the moon and stepped over the side had changed her.

She opened her arms again, but it was to the wolves instead of the sky. "I'm supposed to tell you all something. Something important." She faltered. "But you won't understand like this, will you? You guys should change."

Abel groaned beside him. Seth heard snaps and pops, and realized with a dull shock that his brother was shapeshifting.

One by one, every werewolf changed back into human form. Their bodies jerked. Their spines cracked. Humans emerged where animals had been a moment before. Even Bekah and Levi, who turned out to be sitting near Yasir, resumed their human forms.

When it ended, everyone stood up and looked at each other in confusion, blinking like they had woken up from a very, very heavy sleep.

"What the hell just happened?" Abel asked when he realized he was naked on top of a mountain.

"Holy mother of God," whispered one of the hunters.

"Okay. Here's the message," Rylie said. She didn't yell, but her voice carried over the air anyway. "They said they're sorry. This was never meant to be a curse. But human nature's a tricky thing, and when you try to stick animal souls in with human ones, it gets confusing. So they're sorry. It was a mistake, and they... um, they said they love us." She gave a small, shy smile. "Sorry. That's all I got out of it." She faced the hunters. "Now put down your guns."

Nobody moved. Yasir raised his voice. "You heard the girl. Put down your guns!"

The hunters finally obeyed.

Seth staggered to his feet, and Rylie made her way down the pillars to stand with him and Abel. Everyone kept staring, like they weren't sure what to do without being told. Rylie's skin burned with heat when Seth hugged her. "What was that?" he asked.

"I don't know. I went up there, and it was like... like the moon talked to me. And when I climbed back up, it showed me how to make everyone human again. I think it's just for the night, but... it's over. For now." She bit her bottom lip. "Do I sound crazy?"

"Yes," Seth said.

Abel grabbed Rylie's hand. "What did they look like? What did they sound like?" he asked urgently. "I mean, my God, what does it mean?"

She leaned her head on his shoulder. "I don't know. I'm sorry. I told you everything I've got." She sniffled. "I'm sorry about Eleanor."

"Don't," he said. His eyes were filled with anger, but not at her. "Never, ever be sorry about that."

Yasir climbed up onto the rocks. They all tensed, but he didn't attack.

"What am I supposed to do now?" he asked Seth.

"Why are you asking me?"

"Well, I know what command would tell me," Yasir said. "They would tell me to shoot all the werewolves anyway."

"Command also put my mom in charge," Seth said.

"Yeah. There's that. But our primary mission is to protect humans, and I don't see any werewolves here. Do you?"

They turned to look over the peak of the mountain bathed in moonlight. There weren't as many bodies as Seth originally thought, but there were still too many. The fight had been short and brutal. Three hunters had died. So had a half-dozen werewolves. But the dead wolves were the only animals in sight. Everyone else was very, very human.

Rylie reached out to touch Yasir's arm. He jerked away from her with wide eyes, and she dropped her hand.

"Look… we're all that's left here. Me and Abel and Levi and Bekah… and those guys." She nodded to the naked people among the hunters. "We are the last of all the werewolves. And that's how it should be—I don't want any more. But we don't deserve to die."

"I can't let you run free," he said.

"We have a sanctuary. A place where everyone can learn to be safe and controlled. Let us take everyone home. Nobody else should die." Rylie gave him that look—that one that was so pleading and pathetic that Seth would have done almost anything to make it stop. Yasir didn't look like he was immune to it, either. He wavered under her gaze. "Let us go home."

He faced his men. "Move out! Go back to camp!" Yasir glanced at Seth. "Just so you know, you're not invited to join the Union anymore."

"I'll keep that in mind," he said.

Yasir jumped down, and the hunters slowly cleared out, leaving nothing on the top of Gray Mountain but a very full moon and a dozen very human werewolves.

Epilogue

Home Sweet Home

The drive back to the Gresham ranch didn't feel nearly as long as the drive away had been.

Every window in the Chevelle was rolled down, and a warm summer wind whipped through the car, carrying the fresh aroma of soil and growing wheat. Rylie was curled up under Seth's arm in the backseat, gazing out at the long stretches of empty fields through her hair as it blew in her face. It had been so long since she had smelled cows and other livestock and the distinct strains of pollen that meant *home*.

She tipped her head back to look at Seth. He was gazing out at the farms, too, and he looked as happy as she felt.

He must have felt her gaze, because he glanced down at her. His crooked smile grew. "What are you looking at?"

"Scruffy face," she said, reaching up to rub his chin. "You look like a hobo."

"Oh yeah? *You* look like a hobo."

Neither of them cared that it was the worst retort ever. He bent down to kiss her. "You people are sick," Abel called from the driver's seat.

"Then don't look at us."

"I can hear the lip noises. It's nasty."

Rylie threw an empty wrapper at his head. "You cannot hear that!"

"Can too. Super hearing. And you guys suck face like vacuum cleaners."

Seth rolled his eyes and unbuckled to lean over the front seat and increase the volume on the radio. Abel tried to elbow him in the face, but missed. "There. Fixed it for you."

"Hey! Don't touch the radio! Driver's privilege!"

They responded by kissing very loudly. Abel groaned and made a big deal about it, but it was pretty half-hearted. None of them could seem to stop smiling.

Rylie couldn't think of anything to make the day more perfect except seeing the sign for the Gresham ranch looming ahead of them on the road. She thought that her swelling heart might explode out of her chest. The gray van following them a few car lengths back took the same turnoff they did.

When they met Scott the morning after the moon, they were surprised to find that Stephanie had somehow obtained an old school bus, which was more than enough to transport the surviving wolves to the sanctuary. Nobody argued about getting in once Rylie instructed them to do it, and Stephanie would soon have the survivors under the supervision of the coven.

Rylie had almost joined them, but when Abel found the Chevelle abandoned by Eleanor further down the highway, they decided there was somewhere else they would much rather go.

Dislodging herself from Seth, Rylie leaned out the open window to drink in the familiar sights of the ranch. Not much had changed since she left, aside from the fact that there were no more cattle or goats in the pasture. It was kind of better that way. Smelling the livestock had always made her too hungry.

Gwyn had taken good care of the orchards and garden, though. There were tiny apples growing on the trees. It looked like the lettuce was already coming in.

And when the vehicles pulled around the back of the house, Rylie found Aunt Gwyneth sitting outside the back door. Her silvery hair was twisted into two thick braids, she wore a loose button-up shirt, and her face was shadowed by a cowboy hat.

She saw the Chevelle. Her mouth fell open. She ripped her hat off.

Rylie didn't even wait for Abel to park.

Throwing open the door, she leaped out. "Aunt Gwyneth!" she yelled, launching herself up the hill.

Gwyn didn't have any words to speak. She gripped her niece tightly in her arms, and Rylie squeezed back, doing her very best to keep from crushing her. Her aunt smelled *right*. She was rhubarb pie and steak and garden soil and fertilizer. She was the grass in the field and the sun in the sky.

She was family. She was pack. She was *home*.

Rylie gripped her like she would never let go, but she did have to, eventually. But Gwyn only held her at arm's length. Her aunt's cheeks were shining, and Rylie had left a big wet patch on her shoulder.

"I have so much to tell you," Rylie said. "Oh my gosh, so much has happened, I don't know where to start—I'm so sorry, Gwyn—"

"I don't give a half a damn about your apologies." She sounded gruff, but her eyes gave her away. "Look at you! You've gotten all skinny. Have they been feeding you? I'm going to have a talk with those boys."

"They have taken very, very good care of me," she said with a quavering smile. It lasted about a second before she started crying again, and she had to hug Gwyn some more.

"Hey, don't forget about the rest of us," Seth said, putting a hand on Rylie's shoulder. She backed up a little. He picked Gwyn up off her feet and tried to swing her around.

She pushed him away. "You'll break my back, son." But Rylie could tell she was pleased.

Abel lurked a few feet away, staring at his feet.

"Nice to see you, ma'am," he said.

Gwyn waved her hands. "Don't go all ma'am on me right now. There's plenty of time for that later. Come here." They embraced, and Rylie caught Abel smiling over Gwyn's shoulder. He tried to hide it when he saw her watching. "Now, enough of all this hugging and crying business. Bah!" She gave a hard snort. "You boys been looking after my girl?"

"Yes ma'am," Abel said. She gave him a sharp look.

Seth wrapped his arm around Rylie's waist. "She's been looking after us."

The van doors opened, and Scott climbed out. Bekah and Levi followed after a moment, hanging back like they weren't certain they would be welcome. They were on their way to California, but they had detoured instead of following Stephanie's bus.

"Think you brought a big enough entourage?" Gwyn asked, eyeballing Rylie. She shrugged helplessly. She couldn't do anything about her pack.

"I'm so happy to see you in good health," Scott said, shaking her hand. "How have you been doing?"

Gwyneth's voice took a sharp edge. "I'm well enough, as long as you're not here to kidnap my niece again."

"Aunt Gwyneth!" Rylie gasped. "That was my choice!"

But Scott didn't seem offended. He gave them an apologetic smile. "I have no intent of separating your family again. In fact, the boys tell me you've been trying to sell the ranch. May I ask how that's progressing?"

"We've got a couple offers. I'm considering."

"I hope you would consider one more offer. You see, we've recently come upon a larger 'family' than we expected to have. About a dozen werewolves. Even without Rylie and Abel, my sanctuary in California can only house another eight people. Four more need a place to stay while they work on learning self-control." He swept a hand toward the fields. "With a new fence, and without the livestock, this would be a great place for a new sanctuary. I'd like to buy it."

Gwyn raised an eyebrow. "A werewolf sanctuary?"

"I already promised Scott I would run it," Rylie said helpfully.

"You're sixteen, babe."

"Well, I can run it when I'm not in school." When Gwyn continued to look skeptical, she hastily added, "And Abel could take care of everything when I'm busy doing homework and stuff."

"Could he now?"

Abel shrugged. "It's not like I've got anything else going on."

Gwyn stared at them. Bekah gave her biggest grin from behind Scott's back. Rylie was sure her aunt would say no, but when she finally spoke, it was to say, "Oh, all right. If it keeps you close to home."

Scott and Gwyneth shook hands. Rylie tried not to cheer. She could tell by the way that Seth squeezed her to his side that he felt exactly the same way.

"I don't want to be rude, but we've been driving for quite some time," Scott said. "Would you mind if we rested for a bit?"

"Suppose not, if you don't mind the house being a mess. Most of it's in boxes right now while I get ready to move. Oh, but that reminds me!" Gwyn ducked into the kitchen and reemerged with a stack of envelopes, which she handed to Seth. "The owner of the apartments where you and Abel used to live visited last week with some mail. He asked me to have you set up a forwarding address. Look."

Seth looked through the envelopes. Some of them were really thick. Rylie leaned around his shoulder to read the addresses as he flipped through them.

Some of it was junk, but most of it wasn't. They were packets from universities.

"Oh my gosh," she whispered. "Open one!"

Seth handed Rylie most of the mail, keeping one envelope. He tore it open. His breathing was a little too fast as he skimmed the contents of the letter.

"Don't keep us hanging," Gwyn said. "What's the word?"

"We are pleased to inform you..." he read aloud in a whisper. A huge smile dawned on his face. He spread his arms wide to Rylie. "I got accepted! I'm going to college!"

Gwyn whooped, and Rylie set the letters on a fence post before jumping on Seth. He swung her around with a laugh.

"Look at these," Abel said, going through the rest of the envelopes as they spun. His eyes widened a little more as he looked at each one. "You've been getting them for months."

Seth couldn't seem to stop laughing. He finally put Rylie back on her feet, and she pushed him gently. "Open more!" she urged.

He tore through one after the other. He didn't get accepted to one college—which wasn't his first choice anyway—but the rest were acceptances. Some even included scholarship offers. He was going to have his pick of universities.

Scott shook his hand vigorously. Aunt Gwyn gave him a hug and a peck on the cheek. Even Levi gave him a slap on the back, and he had never really cared that much for Seth.

"This calls for a celebration!" Gwyn declared. "I've still got all kinds of meat in the deep freezer, so let me go thaw some steaks. How's some beer sound to y'all?" She took two steps for the kitchen before thinking about that offer. "Well, for Scott, at least. Rest of you can have well water. It's all I've got."

"I'm almost drinking age," Abel said.

She shot him a look. "*Almost.*"

Scott and his kids hadn't planned on sticking around for long, but they ended up doing a big barbecue on the grill out back. And somehow, before long, the day stretched out into the evening.

Bekah made a run to the store for drinks that didn't have alcohol and got supplies for s'mores, too. They stayed outside until long after the sun set and left crystalline stars in its place. They roasted the marshmallows over the fire and talked about a lot of things, none of which had anything to do with werewolves.

"Believe it or not, you made it back in time for the last week of classes. And graduation, for that matter," Gwyn told Seth as he carefully mashed a chocolate bar against a marshmallow. "The school called. Missing finals means you're not valedictorian, but they might have mentioned something about being salutatorian."

He was still grinning from the college acceptances, but that almost made him light up brighter than the fire. "That's not hard in a graduating class of twenty, is it?"

She kicked him in the ankle. "Keep your sass to yourself. I'm saying congratulations."

"Thank you."

He kissed her on the temple. Gwyn kicked him again before going to talk business with Scott.

"It's going to be fun having a sanctuary out here, huh?" Bekah asked. "It's so nice with all these rolling hills."

"And not a mountain in sight," Levi agreed.

Rylie shared the sentiment. She would have been perfectly happy to never set foot on a mountain again.

She wouldn't have minded if the night kept going forever, but they had been driving for a long time, and eventually, people started yawning. Scott tried to leave for the motel in town, but Gwyn wouldn't hear anything of it.

"If you're buying the ranch, you might as well stay here," she said. "I can even drag in a mattress or two from the shed." Gwyn took Scott, Bekah, and Levi inside to find them sleeping space on the living room floor.

Rylie was exhausted, too, but she didn't want to go inside. Abel was on his sixth or seventh s'more, which seemed to be the only acceptable non-meat food he had encountered since turning into a werewolf. Seth's arm over her shoulders felt so comfortable, so *right*, that she couldn't bear to move him. And the quiet night had filled her with a sense of peace that she hadn't known since her dad had died.

They stayed on the patio swing to watch the fire burn down until there was nothing but glowing embers. Crickets chirped around them in a pulsing rhythm. Muffled conversation drifted through the windows as a breeze ruffled the grass.

"Which college do you think you'll pick?" Rylie asked Seth.

"I don't know. The closest one, I guess. I don't want to go too far."

"Don't do that," she said. "I mean, the closest one is still three hours of driving away. It's not like you could be that close anyway. You should go to your favorite and I'll fly out to visit."

He kissed the top of her head. "I'll figure it out later," he murmured into her hair.

"It kind of sucks," Abel finally said. He had been quiet all night. "I thought we would all get to be together after this, but you've got to go and become some big, important doctor." Seth didn't say anything, but Rylie could see his frown in the dim light of the dying fire. She opened her mouth to protest. Abel spoke first. "But it's good." He hesitated. "I'm proud of you."

Seth grew very still. "Thanks," he said.

"Whatever. Shut up. Don't go all wimpy on me, you ugly jerk." His brother stood up and dusted off his jeans. "I'm wasted. Too much chocolate. I'm going to den up on the softest part of the floor and go unconscious for a few days, but wake me up on the next moon."

"No problem," Rylie said with a half-smile. He went inside, slamming the screen door behind him.

She and Seth continued to swing, very slowly, for a very long time.

The moon seemed so big in the sky. Before getting bitten, she never would have known that it wasn't full, but she could feel the subtle difference in the shadows on the edges. Yet the silvery rays had no pull on her. It wasn't some powerful, immutable force drawing out her wolf. It was just a moon.

Seth was gazing at it, too. "What was it like?" Seth asked. "Talking to gods?"

Rylie gave a faint smile. "Does this mean you believe me?"

"I don't know. I mean, the whole idea is nuts. But I saw you change back to human on a moon. I saw you make everyone else change, too. How do you explain that?"

"It's my animal magnetism," she said with a small giggle.

"You are so hilarious." Seth squeezed her hand. "But I'm serious. What was it like?"

Her smile faded. Her eyes went distant. "It was like... being really warm, and safe. Someone whispered to me. Everything was gray." She shook herself. "I don't know, I can't really remember."

"How do you feel now?"

"Good. Normal." She laughed. "Almost the old normal, even."

"Maybe it's over," he said.

Rylie searched inside herself for the wolf. It was still there, but it was either sleeping or so satisfied that it didn't respond to her internal probe.

"Maybe," she agreed. She nudged a rock off the patio with her toe. "You know... I kind of have to agree with Abel. I mean, I'm happy that you're going to college. But I've still got two more years of high school before I can come, and I just got you back."

Seth wrapped his hand around hers. Their tangled fingers looked right in the moonlight.

"Don't worry about it right now. Right now is good, and I'm not going anywhere yet." He kissed her gently. "We still have all summer."

Buffalo River Regional Library
Columbia, TN 38401

About the Author

SM Reine is a writer and graphic designer obsessed with werewolves, the occult, and collecting swords. Sara spins tales of dark fantasy to escape the drudgery of the desert, where she lives with her husband, the Helpful Toddler, and a small army of black familiars.

Sign up to be notified of new releases!
eepurl.com/eWERY

CPSIA information can be obtained at www.ICGtesting.com
Printed in the USA
LVOW13s1616080814

398214LV00022B/1056/P